the vincent boys

ALSO BY ABBI GLINES

The Vincent Brothers

the vincent boys

ABBI GLINES

Simon Pulse

New York London Toronto Sydney New Delhi

SIMON PULSE
An imprint of Simon & Schuster Children's Publishing Division
1230 Avenue of the Americas, New York, NY 10020
First Simon Pulse hardcover edition October 2012
Copyright © 2012 by Abbi Glines
All rights reserved, including the right of reproduction in whole or in part in any form.
SIMON PULSE and colophon are registered trademarks of Simon & Schuster, Inc.
For information about special discounts for bulk purchases, please contact Simon & Schuster Special Sales at 1-866-506-1949 or business@simonandschuster.com.
The Simon & Schuster Speakers Bureau can bring authors to your live event. For more information or to book an event contact the Simon & Schuster Speakers Bureau at 1-866-248-3049 or visit our website at www.simonspeakers.com.
Designed by Mike Rosamilia
The text of this book was set in Adobe Caslon Pro.
Manufactured in the United States of America
2 4 6 8 10 9 7 5 3 1
This book has been cataloged with the Library of Congress.
ISBN 978-1-4424-8526-6 (hc)
ISBN 978-1-4424-8525-9 (pbk)
ISBN 978-1-4424-8524-2 (eBook)

To my son, Austin. The only person who understands my love of football because he just may love it a little more.

Roll Tide, son.

ACKNOWLEDGMENTS

I have to start by thanking Keith, my husband, who tolerated the dirty house, lack of clean clothes, and my mood swings, while I wrote this book (and all my other books).

My three precious kiddos, who ate a lot of corn dogs, pizza, and Frosted Flakes because I was locked away writing. I promise, I cooked them many good hot meals once I finished.

Tammara Webber and Elizabeth Reyes, my critique partners. Somehow I convinced these ladies to become my critique partners. Now I get to read their books before anyone else! I'd throw in an "I'm just kidding" but, well . . . I'm not. I love their work. It's a major perk. Their ideas, suggestions, and encouragement make the writing process so much easier. They're amazing, and I don't know how I ever finished a book without them.

I'd also like to thank my agent, Jane Dystel, who convinced me I needed an agent and taking a chance on me. She is brilliant, and I'm lucky to have her.

Jennifer Klonsky and the rest of the Simon Pulse staff have all been amazing through this process. As far as publishers go, it doesn't get any better.

My FP girls. I'm choosing not to share what FP stands for because my mother may read this and it will give her heart failure. Kidding . . . maybe. You girls make me laugh, listen to me vent, and always manage to give me some eye candy to make my day brighter. You are truly my posse. What happens in New York City, stays in New York City . . . eh, girls?

the vincent boys

SEVEN YEARS AGO . . .

"You notice anything different about Ash?" my cousin Sawyer asked as he climbed up the tree to sit beside me on our favorite limb overlooking the lake. I shrugged, not sure how to answer his question. Sure, I'd noticed things about Ash lately. Like the way her eyes kind of sparkled when she laughed and how pretty her legs looked in shorts. But there was no way I was confessing those things to Sawyer. He'd tell Ash, and they'd both laugh their butts off.

"No," I replied, not looking at Sawyer for fear he'd be able to tell I was lying.

"I heard Mom talking to Dad the other day, saying how you and me would start noticing Ash differently real soon. She said Ash was turning into a beauty, and things between the three of us would change. I don't want things to change," Sawyer said with a touch of concern in his voice. I couldn't look him at him. Instead I kept my eyes fixed on the lake.

"I wouldn't worry about it. Ash is Ash. Sure, she's always been pretty, I guess, but that's not what's important. She can climb a tree faster than either of us, she baits her own hook, and she can fill up water balloons like a pro. The three of us have been best friends since preschool. That won't change." I chanced a glance at Sawyer. My speech sounded pretty convincing, even to me.

Sawyer smiled and nodded. "You're right. Who cares that she's got hair like some kind of fairy princess? She's Ash. Speaking of water balloons, could you two please stop sneaking out and throwing them at cars right outside my house at night? My parents are gonna catch y'all one of these days, and I won't be able to get y'all outta trouble."

I grinned, thinking about Ash covering her mouth to silence her giggles last night when we'd snuck down there to fill up the balloons. That girl sure loved to break rules—almost as much as I did.

"I heard my name." Ash's voice startled me. "You two better not still be making fun of me about this stupid bra Mama's making me wear. I've had it with the jokes. I'll break both your noses if it doesn't stop." She was standing at the bottom of the tree with a bucket of crickets in one hand and a fishing pole in the other. "Are we gonna fish or had y'all rather just stare down at me like I've grown another head?"

Chapter 1

ASHTON

Why couldn't I have just made it home without seeing them? I wasn't in the mood to play good freaking Samaritan to Beau and his trashy girlfriend. Although he wasn't here, Sawyer would expect me to stop. With a frustrated groan, I slowed down and pulled up beside Beau, who had put some distance between him and his vomiting girlfriend. Apparently, throw up wasn't a mating call for him. "Where's your truck parked, Beau?" I asked in the most annoyed tone I could muster. He flashed me that stupid sexy grin that he knew made every female in town melt at his feet. I'd like to believe I was immune after all these years, but I wasn't. Being immune to the town's bad boy was impossible.

"Don't tell me perfect little Ashton Gray is gonna offer to

help me out," he drawled, leaning down to stare at me through my open window.

"Sawyer's out of town, so the privilege falls to me. He wouldn't let you drive home drunk and neither will I."

He chuckled sending a shiver of pleasure down my spine. God. He even *laughed* sexy.

"Thanks, beautiful, but I can handle this. Once Nic stops puking, I'll throw her in my truck. I can drive the three miles to her house. You run on along now. Don't you have a bible study somewhere you should be at?"

Arguing with him was pointless. He would just start throwing out more snide comments until he had me so mad I couldn't see straight. I pressed the gas and turned into the parking lot. Like I was going to be able to just leave and let him drive home drunk. He could infuriate me with a wink of his eye, and I worked real hard at being nice to everyone. I scanned the parked cars for his old, black Chevy truck. Once I spotted it, I walked over to him and held out my hand.

"Either you can give me the keys to your truck or I can go digging for them. What's it going to be, Beau? You want me searching your pockets?"

A crooked grin touched his face. "As a matter of fact, I think I might just enjoy you digging around in my pockets, Ash. Why don't we go with option number two?"

Heat rose up my neck and left splotches of color on my

cheeks. I didn't need a mirror to know I was blushing like an idiot. Beau never made suggestive comments to me or even flirted with me. I happened to be the only reasonably attractive female at school he completely ignored.

"Don't you dare touch him, you stupid bitch. His keys are in the ignition of his truck." Nicole, Beau's on-again-off-again girlfriend, lifted her head, slinging her dark brown hair back over her shoulder, and snarled at me. Bloodshot blue eyes filled with hate watched me as if daring me to touch what was hers. I didn't respond to her nor did I look back up at Beau. Instead I turned and headed for his truck, reminding myself I was doing this for Sawyer.

"Come on then and get in the truck," I barked at both of them before sliding into the driver's seat. It was really hard not to focus on the fact this was the first time I'd ever been in Beau's truck. After countless nights of lying on my roof with him, talking about the day we'd get our driver's licenses and all the places we would go, I was just now, at seventeen years old, sitting inside his truck. Beau picked Nicole up and dumped her in the back.

"Lie down unless you get sick again. Then make sure you puke over the side," he snapped while opening the driver's side door.

"Hop out, princess. She's about to pass out; she won't care if I'm driving."

I gripped the steering wheel tighter.

"I'm not going to let you drive. You're slurring your words. You don't need to drive."

He opened his mouth to argue then mumbled something that sounded like a curse word before slamming the door and walking around the front of the truck to get in on the passenger's side. He didn't say anything, and I didn't glance over at him. Without Sawyer around, Beau made me nervous.

"I'm tired of arguing with females tonight. That's the only reason I'm letting you drive," he grumbled, without a slur this time. It wasn't surprising that he could control the slurring. The boy had been getting drunk before most the kids our age had tasted their first beer. When a guy had a face like Beau's, older girls took notice. He'd been snagging invites to the field parties way before the rest of us.

I managed a shrug. "You wouldn't have to argue with me if you didn't drink so much."

He let out a hard laugh. "You really are a perfect little preacher's daughter, aren't you, Ash? Once upon a time you were a helluva lot more fun. Before you started sucking face with Sawyer, we use to have some good times together." He was watching me for a reaction. Knowing his eyes were directed at me made it hard to focus on driving. "You were my partner in crime, Ash. Sawyer was the good guy. But the two of us, we were the troublemakers. What happened?"

How do I respond to that? No one knows the girl who used to steal bubble gum from the Quick Stop or abduct the paperboy to tie him up so we could take all his papers and dip them in blue paint before leaving them on the front door steps of houses. No one knew the girl who snuck out of her house at two in the morning to go toilet-paper yards and throw water balloons at cars from behind the bushes. No one would even believe I'd done all those things if I told them. . . . No one but Beau.

"I grew up," I finally replied.

"You completely changed, Ash."

"We were kids, Beau. Yes, you and I got into trouble, and Sawyer got us out of trouble, but we were just kids. I'm different now."

For a moment he didn't respond. He shifted in his seat, and I knew his gaze was no longer focused on me. We'd never had this conversation before. Even if it was uncomfortable, I knew it was way overdue. Sawyer always stood in the way of Beau and me mending our fences, fences that had crumbled, and I never knew why. One day he was Beau, my best friend. The next day he was just my boyfriend's cousin.

"I miss that girl, you know. She was exciting. She knew how to have fun. This perfect little preacher's daughter who took her place sucks."

His words hurt. Maybe because they were coming from him or maybe because I understood what he was saying. It wasn't as if I never thought about that girl. I hated him for making me miss her too. I worked really hard at keeping her locked away. Having someone actually want her to be set loose made it so much harder to keep her under control.

"I'd rather be a preacher's daughter than a drunk whore who vomits all over herself," I snapped before I could stop myself. A low chuckle startled me, and I glanced over as Beau sunk down low enough in his seat so his head rested on the worn leather instead of the hard window behind him.

"I guess you're not completely perfect. Sawyer'd never call someone a name. Does he know you use the word *whore*?"

This time I gripped the steering wheel so tightly my knuckles turned white. He was trying to make me mad and he was doing a fabulous job. I had no response to his question. The truth was, Sawyer would be shocked that I'd called someone a whore. Especially his cousin's girlfriend.

"Loosen up, Ash, it's not like I'm gonna tell on you. I've been keeping your secrets for years. I like knowing my Ash is still there somewhere underneath that perfect facade."

I refused to look at him. This conversation was going somewhere I didn't want it to go.

"No one is perfect. I don't pretend to be," I said, which was a lie and we both knew it. Sawyer was perfect, and I worked hard to be worthy. The whole town knew I fell short of his glowing reputation.

Beau let out a short, hard laugh. "Yes, Ash, you do pretend to be."

I pulled into Nicole's driveway. Beau didn't move.

"She's passed out. You're going to have to help her," I whispered, afraid he'd hear the hurt in my voice.

"You want me to help a vomiting whore?" he asked with an amused tone.

I sighed and finally glanced over at him. He reminded me of a fallen angel as the moonlight casted a glow on his sun-kissed blond hair. His eyelids were heavier than usual, and his thick eyelashes almost concealed the hazel color of his eyes underneath.

"She's your girlfriend. Help her." I managed to sound angry. When I let myself study Beau this closely, it was hard to get disgusted with him. I could still see the little boy I'd once thought hung the moon, staring back at me. Our past would always be there, keeping us from ever really being close again.

"Thanks for reminding me," he said, reaching for the door handle without breaking his eye contact with me. I dropped my gaze to study my hands, which were now folded in my lap. Nicole fumbled around in the back of the truck, causing it to shake gently and reminding us that she was back there. After a few more silent moments, he finally opened the door.

Beau carried Nicole's limp body to the door and knocked. It opened and he walked inside. I wondered who opened the door. Was it Nicole's mom? Did she care her daughter was passed out drunk? Was she letting Beau take her up to her room? Would Beau stay with her? Crawl in bed with her and fall asleep? Beau reappeared in the doorway before my imagi- nation got too carried away.

Once he was back inside the truck, I cranked it up and headed for the trailer park where he lived.

"So tell me, Ash, is your insistence to drive the drunk guy and his whore girlfriend home because you're the perpetual good girl who helps everyone? 'Cause I know you don't like me much, so I'm curious as to why you want to make sure I get home safe."

"Beau, you're my friend. Of course I like you. We've been friends since we were five. Sure we don't hang out anymore or go terrorizing the neighborhood together, but I still care about you."

"Since when?"

"Since when what?"

"Since when do you care about me?"

"That is a stupid question, Beau. You know I've always cared about you," I replied. Even though I knew he wouldn't let such a vague answer fly. The truth was that I never really talked to him much anymore. Nicole was normally wrapped around one of his body parts. And when he spoke to me, it was always to make some wisecrack.

"You hardly acknowledge my existence," he replied.

"That's not true."

He chuckled. "We sat by each other in history all year, and you hardly ever glanced my way. At lunch you never look at me, and I sit at the same table you do. We're at the field parties every weekend, and if you ever turn your superior gaze in my direction, it's normally with a disgusted expression. So I'm a little shocked you still consider me a friend."

The large live oak trees signaled the turn into the trailer park where Beau had lived all is life. The sight of the rich beauty of the southern landscape as you pulled onto the gravel road was deceiving. Once I drove passed the large trees, the scenery drastically changed. Weathered trailers with old cars were up on blocks, and battered toys scattered the yards. More than one window was covered with wood or plastic. I didn't gawk at my surroundings. Even the man sitting on his porch steps with a cigarette hanging out of his mouth and wearing nothing but his underwear didn't surprise me. I knew this trailer park well. It was a part of my childhood. I came to a stop in front of Beau's trailer. It would be easier to believe that this was the alcohol talking, but I knew it wasn't. We hadn't been alone in over four years. Since the moment I became Sawyer's girlfriend, our relationship had changed.

I took a deep breath, then turned to look at Beau. "I never talk in class. Not to anyone but the teacher. You never talk to me at lunch, so I have no reason to look your way. Attracting your attention leads to you making fun of me. And, at the field, I'm not looking at you with disgust. I'm looking at Nicole with disgust. You could really do much better than her." I stopped myself before I said anything stupid.

He tilted his head to the side as if studying me. "You don't like Nicole much, do you? You don't have to worry about her hang-up with Sawyer. He knows what he's got, and he isn't going to mess it up. Nicole can't compete with you."

Nicole had a thing for Sawyer? She was normally mauling Beau. I'd never picked up on her liking Sawyer. I knew they'd been an item in seventh grade for, like, a couple of weeks, but that was junior high school. It didn't really count. Besides, she was with Beau. Why would she be interested in anyone else?

"I didn't know she liked Sawyer," I replied, still not sure I believed him. Sawyer was so not her type.

"You sound surprised," Beau replied.

"Well, I am, actually. I mean, she has you. Why does she want Sawyer?"

A pleased smile touched his lips making his hazel eyes light up. I realized I hadn't exactly meant to say something that he could misconstrue in the way he was obviously doing.

He reached for the door handle before pausing and glancing back at me.

"I didn't know my teasing bothered you, Ash. I'll stop."

That hadn't been what I was expecting him to say. Unable to think of a response, I sat there holding his gaze.

"I'll get your car switched back before your parents see my truck at your house in the morning." He stepped out of the truck, and I watched him walk toward the door of his trailer with one of the sexiest swaggers known to man. Beau and I had needed to have that talk, even if my imagination was going to go wild for a while, where he was concerned. My secret attraction to the town's bad boy had to remain a secret.

The next morning, I found my car parked in the driveway, as promised, with a note wedged under the windshield wipers. I reached for it, and a small smile touched my lips.

"Thanks for last night. I've missed you." He had simply signed it "B."

Chapter 2

ASHTON

Hey, baby. I'm sorry I am just now responding to your
e-mail. Our Internet here is not real dependable and
4G is nonexistent, so my phone is no help. I miss
you like crazy. I think about you all day and wonder
what you're doing. We're spending most of our days
hiking. The trail we took yesterday led to an amazing
waterfall. After five miles uphill in the heat, the ice-
cold water at the falls felt great. I kept wishing you
were here.

It is safe to say my future is not in fishing. I suck at it.
Cade is kicking my tail in catches. He told me yesterday

I needed to stick with football. LOL. I am enjoying my time with him. Thanks for understanding how much I needed to do this. He needs me right now. His big brother will be leaving in a year and I'll be a phone call away, but I won't be there to watch his football practice or help him with his first crush. I'm trying to share all my wisdom with him now.

I love you, Ashton Sutley Gray, so very much. I'm the luckiest guy in the world.

Sawyer

Sawyer,

I figured your delayed response had to do with Internet issues. The connection up in the mountains can't be that great. At least not up in a secluded cabin like y'all are in. I miss you, too. I'm glad you're getting in some big brother time with Cade. I know it means so much to him.

As for me, I am working at the church a good bit. Nothing much to do with you gone. I haven't been going to the field on the weekends. I clean the church mostly, then rent a movie. Leann and Noah are together officially now. When she isn't working, she is with him. So that leaves me without anyone. I'm so used to spending all my time with you. Give Cade and Catherine a hug from me.

I am counting down the days until I see your face again.

Love u bunches,

Ashton

I stared at the computer screen after I clicked send. The fact I hadn't mentioned Beau bothered me a little. I started to tell him about giving Beau and Nicole a ride home. We never really talked about Beau anymore. Sawyer did sometimes when he was worried about him. For most of Sawyer's life he's taken care of Beau. Beau was the son of the Vincent brother who had lived a wild life up until the day he crashed his motorcycle into an eighteen-wheeler. Beau had been in first grade when it happened. I remember his eyes being bloodshot from crying for months. He would sneak out of his trailer and come to my house in the middle of the night. I'd slip outside my window, and we would sit on my roof for hours thinking of things we could do to make him feel better. Normally those ideas would lead to serious mischief that Sawyer had to bail us out of. Sawyer was the son of the good Vincent brother. Sawyer's father had been the oldest of the two Vincent brothers. He had gone to law school and made a fortune defending the average Joe against insurance companies. The town loved Harris Vincent and his beautiful, churchgoing, tennis-playing, junior league-attending wife, Samantha Vincent, and of course their talented, all-American oldest son.

This town wasn't big, and like any small southern town we all knew everyone's business. Their past was common knowledge. Their parents' pasts were no secret. We didn't have secrets in Grove, Alabama. It wasn't possible—well, except maybe at the field. In the dark shadows of the pecan grove that surrounded the large open field where the Mason boys held their famous parties, I'm sure were many secrets. It was the only place where the little ole ladies couldn't watch us from their front porch swings and where the only eyes around were too busy with their own mischief to notice ours.

Reaching over, I picked up the picture Sawyer had framed and given to me of us at a field party last month. His kind smile and bright green eyes made me feel guilty. I hadn't done anything wrong really. I'd just left out the fact I had helped Beau get home safe last night. I should have told him. Setting the picture back down on the desk, I stood up and walked over to the closet to find something to wear. I needed to get out of the house. This summer was going to go by at a snail's pace if I didn't find something to do. My Grana was back home from visiting her sister up in Savannah. I could go volunteer at the nursing home, then go visit Grana. That way, when I e-mailed Sawyer tomorrow, I could tell him I'd gone to the nursing home to see his great-grandmother. He'd like that.

Once I'd done my good deed for the day and visited with Great-Grandma Vincent, I headed to Grana's house. I was anxious to see her. I always missed her like crazy when she was away. With Sawyer and Grana gone, I really had felt all alone. At least she was back now.

The minute my car door closed, Grana's front door opened and out she stepped, grinning and holding a tall glass of sweet iced tea. Her white-blond hair barely brushed her shoulders, and I bit my lip to keep from smiling. We'd had a discussion about the fact she needed to cut her hair before she left. It was getting too long for someone her age. I'd told her so, and she'd waved me off as if I didn't know what I was talking about. Guess she changed her mind. The twinkle in her green eyes told me she knew what I was thinking.

"Well, looky who decided to stop by and visit her Grana. I was beginning to wonder if you were requiring a written invitation these days," she teased. I laughed and walked up the steps to hug her.

"You just got home yesterday," I reminded her. She took a sniff of my shirt and leaned back to look at me.

"Smells like somebody stopped by the old folks home to visit her boyfriend's great-grandmama before she came to see hers."

"Oh, stop it. I was giving you time to sleep in. I know traveling is hard on you."

She took my hand and led me over to sit down beside her on the front porch swing. The diamonds on her fingers glistened against the sunlight. The cold glass she held was pressed into my hands.

"Here, drink this. I poured it as soon as I saw that little car pull in the drive."

I could relax here. This was Grana. She didn't expect me to be perfect. She just wanted me to be happy.

"So you talked to that boyfriend of yours since he's been gone, or are you having you some fun times with another fella while he's away?"

I spewed the tea in my mouth and shook my head as I began to cough. How was it she always knew what was going on when no one else did?

"Well, who is he? He's made you spit tea all over my lap. I at least want a name and a few details."

Shaking my head, I turned so I could look her in the eyes. "There is no one. I got strangled on my tea because you asked me such an insane question. Why would I cheat on Sawyer? He's perfect, Grana."

She made a *hmph* sound and reached over to pat my leg.

"Ain't no man perfect, baby girl. Not a one. Not even your daddy. Although he thinks he is."

She always joked about Daddy being a pastor. He'd been a "hell-raiser" growing up, according to her. When she told me stories about him as a kid, her eyes would light up. Sometimes I could swear that she missed the person he used to be.

"Sawyer's as perfect as it gets."

"Well, I don't know about that. I drove by the Lowry's this morning, and his cousin Beau was out cutting their grass." She paused and shook her head, a big grin on her face. "Girl, there ain't a boy in this town who can hold a candle to Beau Vincent with his shirt off."

"Grana!" I swatted her hand, horrified that my grandmother had admired Beau shirtless.

She chuckled. "What? I'm old, Ashton baby, not blind." I could only imagine how Beau looked shirtless and sweaty. I'd almost had a wreck last week when I'd passed the Green's and he'd been cutting their grass shirtless. It was hard not to look at him. I'd told myself I had just been examining the tattoo on his ribs, but of course I knew the truth. His well-defined abs were really hard to ignore. It just wasn't possible. Then something about the ink on them made his abs even sexier.

"I ain't the only old woman looking. I'm just the only one honest enough to admit it. The others just hire the boy to cut their grass so they can sit at the window and drool."

This was why I loved Grana. Being with her always made me laugh. She accepted life for what it was. She didn't pretend or put on airs. She was just Grana.

"I wouldn't know how Beau looks without a shirt on," I said, which was a lie. "I do know he's nothing but trouble."

Grana clicked her tongue and used her feet to give us a good push. "Trouble can be a lot of fun. It's the straight and narrow that makes life tedious and boring. You're young, Ashton. I'm not saying you need to go out and ruin your life. I'm just saying some excitement is good for the soul."

An image of Beau slouched down in the seat beside me in his truck last night staring at me through his thick curly lashes made my pulse rate increase. He was definitely more than a little excitement. He was lethal.

"Enough about boys. I have one, and I'm not in the market for another. How was your trip?"

Grana smiled and crossed her legs. One high-heeled backless sandal dangled from her hot pink toenails. It was hard to believe she was my straightlaced father's mother.

"We visited. Drank some whisky sours. Caught us a few shows at the theater. That sort of thing."

Sounded like the usual trip to Aunt Tabatha's.

"Did Daddy come by to check on you this morning?"

She sighed dramatically. "Yes, and he of course prayed for my soul. The boy has no sense of adventure."

I smiled into my glass of iced tea. Grana was so much fun.

"You best not repeat that to him either. I have him over here enough, preaching at me." She nudged my leg with hers.

"I never do, Grana."

Grana gave us another push with her foot. "So, if you aren't gonna go find yourself a tattooed sexy bad boy to spend your summer with, then you and I need to do something. Can't have you cleaning the church every day. Where's the excitement in that?"

"Shopping. We could always go shopping," I replied.

"That's my girl. We will shop. But not today. I have to unpack and clean this place up. We will make a date later this week. Just you and me. Maybe we can find us some fellas while we are out."

Shaking my head, I laughed at her teasing comment. She really wasn't a fan of Sawyer. She was the only person in this town who didn't think he walked on water.

After making plans to go shopping with Grana, I headed back to the house.

I'd managed to spend a good part of the day out of my bedroom. I could finish up the rest of the daylight hours with a good book.

Luckily, neither of my parents was home when I pulled into the driveway. When Daddy was home, he would always come up with some job at the church I needed to do. I wasn't in the mood to spend the rest of my day making sure all the pews had a hymnal or wiping down tables in the Sunday school rooms. I just wanted to go read a steamy romance novel and live in the fictional pages for a little while.

The moment I stepped into my bedroom to change out of my clothes, which reeked of disinfectant spray and old people, my phone dinged, alerting me of a text message. Digging into my pocket, I pulled my phone out and stood staring down at the screen as a series of emotions ran through me.

Beau: Meet me at the hole.

The hole was the small lake on the farthest part of Sawyer's property. Beau wanted to meet me out there alone? Why? My heart sped up thinking about what it was Beau was planning. I shifted my eyes to the romance novel I'd been going to read and decided that an afternoon back in the woods with Beau Vincent would be more exciting. Guilt was somewhere inside me, trying hard to beat its way past the sudden wicked need to do something wrong. Before I could come to my senses and change my mind, I replied:

Me: Be there in 15.

My heart hammered against my chest with nervous excitement, or maybe it was the fear of getting caught. I wasn't really doing anything wrong. I mean, Beau was my friend—sort of. He was lonely too. It wasn't like I was going to the hole to make out with him. He probably just wanted to finish the conversation we'd had in his truck last night. He was sober now. More than likely he just wanted to clarify that he hadn't meant for me to take anything the wrong way. It wasn't like we were going to go swimming together or anything.

Beau: Wear a swimsuit.

Okay. Maybe we were going to go swimming. I didn't respond. I wasn't sure what to say. The right thing to do would be to say no. But I always did the right thing. Always. Just this once I wanted to do what I wanted to do. I let the bad girl out just a little.

I walked toward my closet and went for the small bag tucked away on the top shelf. The red bikini I'd bought for Sawyer, but never wore around him for fear he would disapprove, was nestled in the bottom of the shopping bag. So many times I'd reached for the bag but had never actually taken it out. The bikini had been an impulse buy, one I figured would end up rotting away unseen. I could almost see Grana's approving grin as I slowly pulled out the revealing swimsuit she had insisted I buy.

"How's this for trouble, Grana?" I whispered to myself before a small giggle escaped me.

BEAU

If I'd ever taken the time to wonder about my soul being as black as this town seemed to believe, I knew the moment Ashton stepped out of her little white Jetta, looking like an angel from Heaven, that my soul was damned to Hell. When I'd sent the text asking her to meet me, it had been to remind me how untouchable she was. I thought seeing her "no" response would've been the wake-up call I needed to stop obsessing over her. Instead she had agreed, and my stupid black heart had soared. I watched her steps falter when her pretty green eyes met mine. More than anything, I wanted to walk over to her and reassure her I was going to be good. Just talk to her and watch the way her eyes lit up when she laughed or the way she nibbled on her bottom lip when she was nervous. But I couldn't act on that desire. She wasn't mine. She hadn't been mine for a very long time. She shouldn't be here, and I shouldn't have asked. I didn't reassure her, I kept leaning against the tree, looking like the devil and hoping she'd turn and run.

She started walking toward me, and her perfect white teeth caught her full bottom lip between them. I'd fantasized about those lips way too many times. She'd barely covered up her long tanned legs with a pair of shorts that made me want to go to church this Sunday just to thank God for creating her.

"Hey," she said with a nervous blush.

Damn, she was gorgeous. I'd never envied anything of Sawyer's. I loved him like a brother. He was the only family I had truly loved. When he excelled, I silently cheered him on. He'd stood by me through a rough childhood, begging his parents to let me stay over nights when I was too scared to go back to a dark, empty trailer. He'd always had everything I didn't have: the perfect parents, home, and life. But none of that had mattered because I'd had Ashton. Sure, we all three were friends, but Ash had been mine. She'd been my partner in crime, the one person I told all my dreams and fears to, my soul mate. Then just like everything else in Sawyer's perfect life, he got my girl. The only thing I'd thought I could call mine had become his.

"You came," I finally replied. Her blush deepened.

"Yes, but I'm not sure why."

"Me either," I replied since we were being honest.

She took a deep breath and put her hands on her hips. Not a pose she needed to be in with a bikini top being the only thing covering her mouthwatering tits. The view was more stimulation than I needed, so I tore my eyes off her cleavage.

"Look, Beau, I'm bored and lonely with Sawyer gone. Leann is either waiting tables at Hank's or with Noah. I think I'd like to be . . . friends. You were my best friend for eight years of my life. I'd like to find that again."

She wanted us to be friends again? How the hell was I supposed to do that? Wanting her and never being close enough to her to touch her was one thing. She was asking for something I wasn't real sure I could give her. But damned if the pleading look in her eyes didn't have me caving in.

"Okay," I said, grabbing the hem of my shirt and yanking it over my head. "Let's swim."

I didn't wait to see if she'd actually step out of those tiny shorts. Part of me wanted to watch her take them off, but the other part knew my heart couldn't handle watching Ashton shimmying out of the blasted things. My heart may be black, but it was still capable of heart failure.

I grabbed the branch over my head and swung my body up onto it. Standing on the thick limb, I walked out and grabbed the rope swing. For a moment I was a kid again, flying out over the lake. Letting go, I flipped and dove smoothly into the still water. When my head emerged, I turned to look back on the bank in hopes I might catch a glimpse of her undressing. The little shorts were gone and Ashton was walking over to the rope.

This wasn't the first time I'd seen her in a bikini, but it was the first time I'd allowed myself to enjoy the view. My heart began slamming against my chest, but I couldn't take my eyes off her as she climbed up the ladder I'd made years ago out of pieces of wood and nailed into the tree trunk so Ash could climb the tree. She walked slowly out onto the branch and smirked down at me before grabbing the rope and swinging out over the water. After making a perfect spiral, she made one complete flip and dove into the water. It had taken me three long afternoons to teach her how to flip off the rope swing and land smoothly into the water. She'd been eight years old and determined to do everything Sawyer and I did.

Ashton's head emerged from the water and tilted back as her hands smoothed the wet curls out of her face. "It isn't as cold as I'd hoped," she said, grinning triumphantly.

"It's ninety-six degrees and rising today. Before the month is over, this will feel like bathwater." I made an attempt not to appear mesmerized by the way her long eyelashes got all spiky when they were wet.

"Yes, I remember. I've spent as many summers in this lake as you have . . . ," she said, trailing off as if to remind us both whose lake we were swimming in. I wanted her to be comfortable with me. If talking about Sawyer would help, then I'd talk about him. Besides, it wouldn't hurt to keep reminding myself who she belonged to.

"Point taken. Sorry, this new Ashton doesn't resemble the Ash I once knew. I sometimes forget Sawyer's perfect girlfriend is the same girl who used to start mud fights with me up there on the bank."

Ashton's easy smile quickly turned into a frustrated pout.

"I wish you'd stop acting like I'm a different person, Beau. I grew up, but I'm still the same girl. Besides, you changed too. The old Beau wouldn't have completely ignored me because he was too busy making out with his girlfriend to acknowledge my existence."

There were a lot of things I could say to that, but I knew I shouldn't. Because of Sawyer. I had to keep this friendly.

"No, but the old Beau wasn't horny," I shot back with a wink, and splashed water in her face.

Her familiar laughter made my chest ache a little.

"Point taken. I guess having someone built like Nicole all over you is a little distracting. I can see where an old friend would rank under getting laid."

If I'd known Ashton wanted my attention at any point, I would have pushed Nicole aside and given Ashton my undivided attention. But most of the time she was wrapped in Sawyer's arms, and I needed the distraction Nicole provided—something else I couldn't ever admit to Ashton.

"Nicole isn't very modest," I replied, trying to lay the blame on her.

The dimple I'd been fascinated with since the day I'd met Ashton appeared as she gave me a full smile.

"Nicole doesn't even know the definition of the word *modest*. Now the word *vulgar*, I'm pretty sure she's got a grasp on its definition."

Was it my wishful thinking or did she sound jealous of Nicole? Damn, why did the idea of Ashton being jealous make me so freaking happy?

"Nicole's not so bad. She just goes after what she wants," I replied, wanting to test Ashton's reaction.

An annoyed frown came over her face and she stiffened. I couldn't keep the smile from forming on my lips. I liked the fact it bothered her when I defended Nicole. I liked the idea of her feeling anything more than friendship toward me, even if I'd never be good enough for her. I'd never be Sawyer, but knowing she cared just a little bit felt real good.

"You've got bad taste in women, Beau Vincent," she replied. I watched her swim over to the pier and pull herself out to sit on the edge, giving me an extremely pleasant view of her barely covered ass. It took me a minute to remember what we'd been talking about. Ashton's wet body on display was all my lust-addled brain seemed to be focused on. I shook my head to clear my thoughts and remembered her comment about my bad taste in women. If she only knew.

"I suppose Sawyer has better taste?" I asked, and swam

over to join her. She frowned and bit her bottom lip. That hadn't been the response I was expecting. I'd meant to make her smile.

"Maybe because I don't rape him in public, but we both know he could do better."

What the hell did that mean?

"You think so?" I managed to sound casual when all I wanted to do was demand to know who had made her feel as if she wasn't good enough for Sawyer.

She glanced over at me with a sad little smile. The late afternoon sun was directly behind her, causing the long, blond curls framing her face to softly glow. The effect made her resemble the angel she appeared to be. Untouchable unless you were the perfect Sawyer Vincent.

"I'm not blind, Beau. I'm not saying I think I'm ugly. I know I'm passably cute. I've got good hair and my complexion isn't bad. I don't have big, blue eyes or long lashes, but my eyes aren't bad. I'm not exactly exciting or striking. Sawyer is perfect. It's hard to believe he wants me sometimes."

I turned away from her, afraid the incredulous expression on my face would tell her more than she needed to know. I wanted to tell her how her green eyes made guys want to defend her or the way her sweet, pink lips were mesmerizing or how that one single dimple caused my pulse rate to increase. I wanted to point out how those long, tanned legs caused guys to trip over themselves, and when she wore tight shirts, I fought the urge to go cover her up so every male who saw her wouldn't go home and jack off with her image in their head. But I couldn't say any of those things. Forcing my expression to remain casual, I glanced back at her. "I don't think you give yourself enough credit. Sawyer didn't just choose you because of your looks." That's all I needed to say.

She sighed and leaned back on her hands. I had to turn my head away from her again before my eyes could zero in on her tits. I didn't need to study them to know they were perfectly round, soft, plump, and tempting as hell.

"I'm not always good. I try really hard to be good. I want to be worthy of Sawyer—I really do—but it's like there is this other me inside who's trying to get out. I fight it, but I'm not good at it all the time. Sawyer has to keep me in line."

Keep her in line? Wait . . . what? Shaking my head to clear my thoughts from how sweet her nipples would taste, I forced myself to focus on what she was saying instead of how she would taste. She didn't think she was good enough for Sawyer? Had Sawyer made her think something was wrong with her? Surely, he didn't know she felt this way.

"Ash, you've been nothing but perfect since you decided to grow up. Sure, you used to help me put frogs in people's mailboxes, but that girl's gone. You wanted to be perfect, and you achieved it."

She laughed and sat back up. I chanced a glance over at her.

The dimple was there tucked into her cheek as she gazed down at the water.

"If you only knew" was all she said.

"Tell me." The words were out of my mouth before I could stop them.

"Why?"

Because I want you. Just you. The girl I know is in there hiding from the world. I want my Ash back. I couldn't say it like that. She'd see too much. I had to protect myself.

"Because I'd like to know you aren't so perfect. I'd like to know the girl who I once knew was still in there somewhere."

She laughed again and pulled her legs up to rest her chin on them.

"There's no way I'm admitting all my faults to you. Considering most of them are just in my thoughts and I've never acted on them."

What I would give to know what bad thoughts Ashton kept locked away. I doubted they were anything as bad as I wanted them to be. But hell, just a little bit of naughty would drive me crazy.

"I'm not asking for your deep dark secrets, Ash. I just want to know what you could possibly do wrong that makes you feel that Sawyer's got to keep you in line."

Her cheeks turned pink, but she kept her eyes straight ahead. She wasn't going to tell me. I hadn't really expected her to. Ashton had been hiding inside herself for years now. It still hurt so fucking bad when I thought of the girl I'd lost. The one she wouldn't let me see anymore. After a few minutes of silence, I stood up and stretched. I couldn't do this. I built a wall three years ago to keep from getting hurt. Only Ashton held the power to hurt me. I couldn't let her do it again.

"That's fine," I said. "I don't really need you to tell me how you don't always remember to take the buggy back to the return place in the parking lot or you don't make it to the nursing home every week."

I started to walk away, angry at myself for sounding like a jerk but needing to get the hell away from her. This had been a mistake. A big-ass mistake that I was going to pay for.

"Those are things Sawyer has to help me remember. . . . But I wasn't exactly referring to them."

She said it so softly I almost didn't hear her. I should keep walking. I needed to stop this. But I never did the right thing. I turned back around to look at her. She was peering up at me through her wet eyelashes.

"I'm just like any other teenage girl. I envy Nicole because she can be who she wants to be. I can't. But it isn't Sawyer's fault. I've never been able to give in to those urges. My parents expect me to be good."

What the *hell*?

"You want to be like Nicole?" I asked in horror.

She laughed and shook her head.

"Not exactly. I don't desire to vomit on myself and be carried inside my house drunk . . . or be known as a slut. But just once I'd like to know what it feels like to do more than just kiss. To be touched." She stopped and turned her gaze back toward the water. "Maybe to know what the thrill of sneaking out of my house feels like or how it feels to be wanted by someone so desperately they can't help themselves when they kiss me. Maybe to just feel desirable." She stopped again and covered her face with both her hands. "Please forget I said all that."

Talk about an impossible request. I was having a hard enough time breathing. Ah, fuck it all to hell. I was screwed. I needed to remember Sawyer. I loved him. He was my family. He was an idiot for not kissing every damn spot on Ashton's sexy little body and enjoying the gift he had. But he was still my family. I couldn't do this.

She let her hands drop away from her face and turned her guilt-ridden expression back up toward me. The lost look in her eyes was killing me. I wanted to assure her nothing was wrong with her. I wanted to promise to show her exactly how insane she made me. I could show her in five minutes just how desirable she was.

She stood up.

"So now you know my secrets, Beau. Just like old times. I

think that makes us friends again, huh?" The smile on her lips trembled.

Fuck me.

"Yeah, I'd say it does." I replied as regret consumed me.

Chapter 3

ASHTON

I watched as my parents' minivan backed out of the driveway before I picked up my phone and texted Beau.

> Me: Would u like to come watch a movie at my house?

My heart started racing in my chest. What was I doing? I'd already blurred the lines today at the hole. I should have never talked with Beau about secret desires. But just thinking about the intense gleam in his eyes as I'd explained what I wanted to experience made my body flush with excitement.

> Beau: Ur parents?

He knew my parents well enough to know they would never be okay with me spending time with him. I hated how everyone assumed the worst about Beau. Just because his momma was trash didn't mean he was. He had the same blood in him that Sawyer did.

Me: Out of town 2night

My dad had planned a surprise weekend getaway for my parents' anniversary. I'd known about it for a week, but he'd just told my mom this afternoon. They were both safely on the road to Birmingham now.

My phone rang, startling me so badly that I dropped it. Scrambling to pick it up, I worried it may be Sawyer. I'd never be able to keep the guilt out of my voice if I had to talk to him.

It was Beau.

"Hello?" I said.

"I'll leave my truck at the park and walk to your house through the woods. Unlock the back door for me."

He didn't want anyone to see his truck here. I knew it was for my benefit, but it was probably best he didn't park outside my house. He was just my friend, but . . . he was also a boy. A bad boy. Ashton Gray didn't have bad boys over while her parents were away.

"Okay, if that's what you want to do."

"It is." His deep voice made me feel tingly inside.

"I'll see you in a little while then," I replied.

"Yeah," he said before he hung up. I stared down at the phone; I was torn between excitement and fear. I was going to get to spend more time alone with Beau. I'd missed him. Being able to be honest with someone was nice. I didn't have to pretend. Then there was also the fact I liked the way his eyes sent shivers over my body as he stared at me. There was something wicked about Beau that drew me to him. What was wrong with me? Why did I want to sin so badly?

I dropped the phone on my bed and headed to the shower. I wouldn't think about the rule I was breaking. This wasn't anything bad. It was a small rule if you thought about rules in general. I mean there were bigger rules I could break. Besides I needed to break some rules before I went crazy.

A light knock on the back door sent the butterflies flapping around in my stomach into a frenzy. I heard the latch on the door as it opened and closed. I quickly slipped on a white eyelet sundress after trying on several other more casual outfits; I'd decided I wanted to look nicer. The sundress was short, with spaghetti straps, so it looked casual enough for a movie night. Maybe . . . sort of. I studied my feet. I'd just painted my toes cotton candy pink and decided to stay barefoot. Even more casual.

I headed down the hall to greet my guest. The air entering my lungs was stalled when I saw Beau standing in the kitchen.

Black had always looked good on him, but having him stand in my kitchen in a tight black T-shirt and a pair of low-riding jeans made me a little dizzy. When my vision began to blur, I realized I was holding my breath.

"Hey," I managed to say, mentally cringing at the breathless sound in my voice.

He nodded and gave me a small smile before walking over to the fridge and opening it.

"I'm thirsty. Can I have a Coke?" he asked without looking back at me.

"Um, yeah, sure. I ordered pizza too. It should be here in a few minutes. If you're hungry."

He closed the fridge door, opened the can of Coke in his hand, and then took a swig.

"I'm always hungry," he replied.

"Okay, good." I didn't know what else to say. I'd invited Beau to my house to watch a movie. Now he was here, filling up my house with his sexiness, and I didn't know what to say. He walked toward me, grinning.

"Relax, Ash. It's just me." He nodded his head toward the living room. "Let's go see what kind of movie selection you've got these days."

Swallowing nervously, I turned and headed to the living room. This was a bad idea. I was acting like an idiot. This wasn't the way friends acted. If I wanted him to be my friend, I needed to start acting like one and not a love-struck moron.

"I rented two movies from the Redbox. If you don't like either, you can pick from the ones I have in my room, but I'm warning you now that they are mostly romantic comedies. The ones I rented are probably more your speed."

I kept my back to him because my cheeks were getting warm and I hated the idea of him seeing me blush. I was being so silly. I reached for the two action movies I'd rented and started to turn around to show him when he moved in behind me. I froze. My body went on high alert, and I took several gulps of air.

"Let me see." His mouth was surprisingly close to my ear. Then his arm reached around me and he snatched the movies from my grasp. When our hands brushed, I sucked in a quick breath. For a second he paused then moved away quickly. My crazy behavior had to be making him uncomfortable.

"Good choice. I've been wanting to see both of these, but Nicole and I don't usually watch movies."

Nicole's name was like a bucket of cold water. He was subtly reminding me he wasn't here for anything more than a movie with a friend—which was true. I just needed to stop lusting after him and everything would be fine.

I pivoted around on the balls of my feet. "Okay, good. Well, pick one and put it in. I'm going to go get my money before the pizza gets here."

But first I am going to splash cold water on my face and calm down,

I thought. I didn't wait for his response before I fled the room.

The doorbell rang while I was shuffling through my purse for money. The delivery guy would probably be someone from school. Beau answering the door didn't seem like the best idea. I rushed out of my bedroom door and came face-to-face with Beau. Or, more accurate, face to chest. A very yummy-smelling chest. I closed my eyes tightly and took a deep breath.

"I'll wait here while you pay," he said in a low whisper. I nodded and stepped around him.

The moment I opened the door, I was instantly relieved Beau was hiding. It was a starting lineman on the football team named Jimmy Noles.

"How's it going, Ashton?" Jimmy asked, smiling.

"Um, good, thanks."

"I guess you're missing Sawyer."

I nodded. "Yes, I am." I handed him the money, "Keep the change, and thanks."

His grin got bigger. "Cool, thanks, Ashton. See ya around."

I returned his smile and closed the door.

Beau stepped out of the hallway. "That smells good."

It did smell good, but I doubted I could actually eat. Beau took the box out of my hand and walked over to the couch and set it down in front of him on the coffee table.

"I'll get some paper plates," I said wishing I didn't sound so nervous.

He started opening the box. "Don't get one for me, but a paper towel would be good."

"Okay," I replied on my way to the kitchen without looking back at him.

Once I got back to the living room, Beau was already on his second slice of pizza. I'm glad he didn't feel awkward by my crazy behavior.

"I went ahead and put the movie in," he said nodding his head toward the television.

"Okay, that's fine," I replied as I reached for a piece of pizza. Beau's attention was on the movie, so eating should have been easy, but it wasn't. I gave up trying to finish my first piece. My nerves wouldn't allow me to eat very much. Beau finally leaned forward and grabbed a paper towel. He wiped his hands then leaned back on the sofa with his eyes still on the movie. I put my plate down on a stack of *Garden & Gun* magazines my dad kept on the coffee table.

"I left you two more pieces. You can't be full."

I glanced over at him. "You mean you didn't stop eating because you were full?"

He shook his head. "No, I was being considerate. I'm never full."

I leaned back on the sofa. "Eat all you want. I'm done."

He didn't lean forward to grab another slice like I had expected him to. Instead his attention stayed on me.

"Why did you invite me here tonight, Ash?"

My face flushed. Why had I asked him to come? Answering that question wasn't easy. Since he'd walked in the door, I'd been acting ridiculous. I never seemed to be at a loss for things to say to Sawyer. Beau rattled me. Now he was being bored to death by the preacher's daughter when he could be spending his evening with his sexy, hot girlfriend, doing all those things I knew nothing about. I was depriving him of an exciting night. The idea that he'd come tonight to entertain me for his cousin's sake made me feel awful. He'd been doing this as a charity, and I couldn't even make it interesting for him. Well, at least I'd fed him.

"I'm sorry. I guess I just didn't want to be alone, but I'm okay. You can go. I know this is dull compared to your normal activities." I managed a weak smile.

His frown deepened as he leaned forward and rested his elbows on his knees, but he didn't take his eyes off me.

"Being with you isn't dull. You just seem uncomfortable. If you want me to leave, I will. I have a feeling you're rethinking the having me over thing."

I sighed and let out a small laugh.

"No. I want you to stay. I've just never had any guy over here but Sawyer, and even then my parents were here. I'm nervous. It's not that I don't want you here."

"Why do I make you nervous?" he asked, watching me.

"I don't know," I answered truthfully.

"Hmm, you're wrong, by the way," he replied, grinning.

"What?"

"You've had other guys here. I use to come here often. Your room still looks the same."

I smiled. He was right. I just needed to remember this was the same boy who used to lie on my bed with me and watch movies.

He closed the space between us and relaxed as he stretched his arm along the back of the sofa. "I don't bite, Ash. It's just me. Promise. Come here and see."

I studied the crook of his arm; the idea of snuggling up against him was extremely tempting. But I didn't think he had that in mind. So instead I leaned back on the couch, careful not to touch him.

His hand didn't come around me and pull me closer. It remained on the back of the couch, and I hated that I was disappointed.

"Relax and watch the movie," he said in a soft voice I'd never heard him use before. It made me feel warm and safe.

Beau's arm eventually slid down to settle on my shoulders. Absently he started tracing small circles on my upper arm. It was almost as if little jolts of electricity were zinging through my body. I hoped he couldn't tell my breathing was getting erratic. I closed my eyes and fantasized about how it would feel to run my hands under his T-shirt and touch the soft skin that covered his muscled chest. I glanced up at him through my lashes, and his attention was completely focused on the movie.

He had no idea he was driving me crazy.

I slowly moved closer to him until my head was nestled in the crook of his arm. The smell of Irish Spring soap and the outdoors filled my senses. Sawyer always smelled like cologne. I liked soap. I turned my head just enough so I could smell him better. His arm gently tightened around me. He didn't mean anything by it, but it felt so very good. I turned my body toward his side and closed my eyes. My imagination took over, and I wondered what it would feel like if he didn't have this bothersome shirt covering his chest.

"Ash." Beau's voice entered my fantasy.

"Hmm . . ." I managed to respond as my hand touched his abs.

"What're you doing?" His voice didn't sound right. There was a panicked tone to it that snapped me out of my dream and into reality. I gasped when I realized my leg was hiked up on Beau's thigh. The hem of my sundress was barely covering my panties. To make matters worse, my hand was under his black shirt; his skin felt so warm and soft. The soft, circular patterns on my arm had stopped, and his hand was no longer touching me. Horror washed over me, and I jerked my hand out of his shirt and sat up.

"Oh my God," I blurted out. "I'm sorry. . . . I didn't mean . . . I'm sorry." I couldn't look at him. Not after I'd been all over him! Instead I did the only thing I could think of: I ran for my room.

I pushed the door hard enough to slam it, but the loud crack never came.

"Ash, wait." Beau's voice made me cringe. *Oh God, why did he have to follow me? Couldn't he have just left?*

I couldn't face him.

"I'm sorry. Just . . . go, okay?" I crossed my arms and stared hard at the window, waiting for him to leave. His arms wrapped around me from behind, and I whimpered as the humiliation just got worse. He was going to try to comfort me.

"I don't know what's going on in that head of yours, but from the way you're acting, I can imagine it's pretty bad." He lowered his head to my shoulder. "You want me to leave and I'm going to go. But first I want to make sure you understand something."

My throat was tight and sobs constricted my airway. Responding wasn't possible.

"I started that in there. Not you. I wasn't prepared for the reaction I got. I thought you'd push me away—not . . . snuggle closer." He stopped again, and his breath was warm on my neck as his lips touched my bare shoulder. I shivered, and his hands ran down my arms until they covered mine. "I shouldn't have touched you. But I couldn't help myself," he murmured into my ear.

I wanted to argue. It wasn't his fault. I wanted to tell him I was the one who got carried away. But I couldn't manage more than just a small snivel. "I can't do this, Ash. God knows I want to, but I can't." And then he was gone. I turned to see him walking out my door. More than anything, I wanted to call him back. But I didn't.

Chapter 4

ASHTON

The ding alerting me of a text message woke me up. I rubbed my eyes and tried to focus before reaching for my phone. The message was from Beau.

> Beau: G'morning.

The shock of seeing his name on my phone this early had me sitting up quickly and then flopping back down against my pillow as last night's events rushed back to me. I could almost feel Beau's lips on my shoulder, and I shivered under the covers.

> Beau: When u wake up, call me.

I should ignore him. I should ignore these texts and pretend like last night never happened. But the memory of his breath in my ear and his hands caressing my arms threw all my good intentions out the window.

Me: I'm awake now.

In less than a minute my phone rang. I had a decision to make and fast. I needed to either ignore his call and save both Beau and me the future trouble or answer and not care about the consequences.

"Hello."

"Hey." His voice made me instantly glad I had answered.

"About last night—" I began.

"I want to see you today," he interrupted.

My heart pounded in my chest and I smiled up at the ceiling. He wanted to see me.

"Okay," I replied quickly.

"Do you mind coming here?"

"Your place?" I asked.

"Yeah, I've got some things I need to do for Mom. Why don't you come keep me company?"

I sat up in bed, grinning like an idiot.

"I'll be there in thirty minutes. Have you eaten?"

"No, not yet."

"I'll bring breakfast then," I replied.

"Sounds good."

"Okay, bye."

He hesitated for a moment then said, "See ya soon."

My heart was going at warp speed as I jumped up and headed to the kitchen to make some biscuits before taking a shower.

BEAU

I reached for my phone—for at least the tenth time—to call and cancel when Ashton's Jetta spun into the gravel driveway outside.

Great.

I'd successfully fought off my good intentions just long enough for her to get here. This was bad. Hurting people isn't something I have issues with, but hurting Sawyer? That's out of the question.

Ashton stepped out of her car wearing another short dress and carrying a plate of food. Watching the sway of her hips under the wispy fabric as she made her way toward me, the corners of her mouth turned up in a shy little smile, I decided I didn't care if I was being a dirtbag. Sawyer wasn't here, and I couldn't seem to help myself.

My cousin should have kept his ass home.

"I made sausage biscuits," she said as she approached the door.

"Yum, I'm starving," I replied, holding the door open for her. The breeze ruffled her hair as she walked past me. Why did she have to smell so damn good? I closed the door and turned around to drink her in. Last night when I'd left her, I'd gone straight to Nicole. Reminding myself who I was had been vitally important. Nicole had been very willing, but my body hadn't been able to forget how good Ashton had felt curled up against me.

"I didn't expect you to call me," Ashton said softly while studying the plate of biscuits in her hands.

I'd had a moment of intense weakness when I'd woken up from an incredibly good dream she had starred in. All I could think about was being near her again.

"I hated the way we left things last night."

She blushed and glanced up at me. "I'm really sorry about how I acted."

Damn, damn, damn, I wasn't going to be able to resist her. Pushing Sawyer to the deep, dark forgotten part of my mind, I walked over to her, took the plate of biscuits, and put them down on the counter.

"I told you last night: I started it. I should be the one apologizing."

She let out a small laugh and stared down at her feet. "No, I distinctly remember it being my leg that was hiked up in your lap and my hand that was up your shirt. You had completely stopped touching me. Thanks for trying to take the blame off me, but I was there, Beau."

I slipped my arms around her waist and pulled her to me. Right now I didn't care who she belonged to. I wanted her and I couldn't see past my need.

"Look at me," I whispered, slipping my finger under her chin and tilting her face up so I could see her eyes. "The only reason I didn't grab you and haul you onto my lap last night was because for the first time in my life, I want something that belongs to the only person I love. I started touching you last night because I couldn't keep my hands off you. I thought if I could touch you just a little bit, I'd be able to handle it. But then you didn't react the way I expected." I stopped and closed my eyes. Staring down at her while I talked about her reaction to my touch was difficult. Those big, innocent green eyes soaked in every word out of my mouth. God, she was perfect.

"And my good intentions were fading fast. If you'd kept touching me for just a few more seconds, I'd have lost it. I was hanging on by a thread. A very thin thread."

She stepped back out of my embrace and gave me a little grin.

"Okay. Thank you for saying that." She turned and walked over to the counter then began taking the plastic wrap off the biscuits.

"We both love him. Neither of us wants to hurt him. But . . . we're drawn to each other. We have history. The three of us. For the past few years, it's been just me and Sawyer. I didn't want it to be that way; it just happened. I think we can all be friends again. I want us to be. So while he's gone, let's just enjoy being friends. I promise to keep my hands to myself if you promise the same."

She peered at me over her shoulder as she moved to set the biscuits on plates she'd found in the dish rack. Telling her how I'd do anything she asked wasn't exactly the best move. I nodded and went to get glasses and orange juice so we could eat breakfast together. Just like we use to.

After breakfast I convinced Ashton to help me wash my truck. I figured any reason to get her outside and in public so that I wouldn't be tempted to haul her back to my bedroom was a good idea.

"Stop it, Beau!" Ashton squealed as she ran around the side of the truck and away from the water hose I'd aimed her way.

"But you've got soap all over your arms. I'm just trying to wash it off," I replied. Her laughter made something inside me tighten, and I forced myself not to think about it.

"Sure you were. By soaking me. I'd prefer the soapy arms, thank you very much."

"Ah, come on, Ash. I was just trying to help. I promise I won't do it again. Besides, you aren't even wearing a white shirt. I've got no reason to hose you down."

She walked cautiously around the front of my truck. She

didn't trust me. I dropped the hose and held up both my hands. "See, I promise," I assured her.

She tilted her head to one side and bit her bottom lip. "Hmm, okay."

I watched her slowly approach the bucket of soapy water to retrieve the sponge she'd dropped. Before I could respond, she stood up and hurled a large wet soapy sponge at my face and squealed in delight before turning and running back to the other side of the truck.

"You've asked for it now!" I yelled at her, and took off around the opposite side of the truck to catch her.

"I'm sorry!" she screamed through her laughter.

"Too late for apologizes, darlin'. I'm taking you down."

"Beau, I promise I won't! Please don't throw it at me." She ducked down behind the back of the truck.

"Well, isn't this sweet?"

Nicole's voice caught me off guard. I stopped chasing Ashton and tossed the wet sponge into the bucket before turning around to find Nicole leaning up against her mother's candy-apple red Camaro. The scowl on her face was directed toward Ashton. I glanced back to see Ashton standing beside the bed of my truck, holding the soaking-wet sponge in her hands and studying Nicole nervously. The comparison of the two girls was like night and day: Where Nicole fit into this run-down trailer park, Ashton looked completely out of place. Old man Macklery stepped out of his front door with a beer in his hand, yelling over his shoulder at his wife before slamming the door. Everything around me faded away when I was with Ashton. It was no wonder I'd missed Nicole's arrival. Turning back to Nicole, I shot her a warning glare.

"I didn't hear you drive up."

She raised her eyebrows and shifted her angry gaze toward me. I knew why she had stopped by. The skin-tight miniskirt and halter top that barely covered her boobs meant she'd come over looking for some action.

"You were having a little too much fun to notice anything but her."

Crap! This wasn't good. Ashton was the one person Nicole felt threatened by. It didn't matter how nice Ashton had always been to Nicole. Nicole hated her. Catching her soaking wet in a skimpy little sundress washing my truck didn't look real inno-cent. Ashton was sexy as hell, all wet and soapy, a fact I knew wouldn't go unnoticed by Nicole. She would love to see Ashton crash and burn. I needed to say something, but I couldn't think of anything that would fix this.

"Hello, Nicole," Ashton said, breaking the tense silence. "It's past time for me to leave. I'm glad you're here to take my place."

I studied the worried frown tugging at the corners of her mouth. If shoving Nicole back into her Camaro and forcing her to leave would make those pretty lips smile and laugh again, I would. Ashton's eyes met mine and she gave me a bright smile: the kind she used to give me, the kind she had to force. Not the smile I'd grown accustomed to the over last few days.

"I'll let Sawyer know I checked in on you and entertained you in his absence like he requested. Looks like you have someone who'll no doubt be much more your speed here now," she said, staring back at me. Then she swung her attention toward Nicole and blasted her with the same fake smile.

"Have fun, you two." She waved to Nicole. "See ya around."

I watched as Ash walked to her car and slipped inside, dripping wet. I wanted to run after her and beg her not to leave, but I knew this was her way of saving our butts with Sawyer. I hadn't been able to think of anything to say, and I'd left all the explaining up to her.

"I find it hard to believe Sawyer meant for her to come over here and have a soapy water fight with you," Nicole said as she walked toward me.

"Shut up," I replied, and bent over to pick up the hose so I could rinse off my truck.

"I hate her, Beau. You know that. If she needs babysitting, someone else can do it. She isn't your concern."

"You don't tell me who I can and can't spend time with, Nicole."

"Hell yes, I do! The last time I checked, we're an item. You're mine. I don't want you around her. Stay the fuck away from her, or I'll tell Sawyer just how friendly you two were when I drove up. I'm not blind, Beau. I saw the way you were looking at her. The girl might as well have been naked."

I swung my head around and glared at her. "No one threatens me, Nicole. You know better. Don't make that mistake."

"So what, you can paw your cousin's girlfriend and I just have to sit and take it?"

"I wasn't pawing her. We were washing my truck. We're friends, Nicole. She was my best friend growing up. Our being friends now is not a big deal, and Sawyer's okay with it. Ashton's too good for me. She knows that. I know that. Sawyer knows that. You should know that."

Nicole didn't say anything. I started rinsing off the truck, hoping this conversation was over.

"But you like her?"

It didn't sound like a question. More like a statement.

"Yes, Nicole. She's my cousin's girlfriend. She's nice and kind and everything we aren't. Everyone likes her. Everyone but you."

"I mean you like her, like her. The way you were looking at her. You want her."

There were a million things I wanted to say. But saying any of them would be a bad move. Keeping Nicole's mouth shut was more important.

"She's Sawyer's girl."

Chapter 5

ASHTON

"Oh come on, it'll be fun!" Leann assured me for the hundredth time.

I scowled at her back as she got out of the car. Somehow she'd managed to drag me to the Masons' field. When she'd asked me to hang out with her that night, I'd thought she meant a movie and maybe shopping. I hadn't thought she meant to bring me to the field. I stopped boring holes into her back and glanced over at Beau's parked truck. I hadn't heard from him since I'd left him and Nicole at his trailer. At first I'd expected him to text or call, but after twenty-four hours I began to realize I wouldn't be hearing from him. Nicole hadn't seemed very happy about me being there. I should've expected this reaction.

"Come on, Ashton." Leann opened my car door and smiled down at me. Her short, curly brown hair bounced as she waved her arm out toward the field.

"There's a life outside of Sawyer Vincent. I swear there is," she teased while adjusting her black-framed glasses that had slid down her nose. Only Leann could make glasses look chic.

"I know that." She had no idea how much I knew that. "But coming to the field without Sawyer seems pointless. I mean, Noah will be here soon, and I'll be the third wheel."

"Nonsense. Noah will be both our dates." She flashed me a grin and pulled me into the clearing.

The bonfire and music were already pumping. The smell of burning pecan wood filled the night air. Different groups gathered around the lit-up clearing as some couples were already making their way into the privacy of the shadows within the trees. I walked beside Leann, listening to her chatter on and on about the new truck Noah had bought. I'd been trying so hard to ignore my surroundings and everyone around me that I was caught by surprise when Leann sat down on a log and pulled me down beside her.

"Look who I pulled out of hiding," Leann announced to the group.

"Ashton. She lives," Ryan Mason called out from across the fire, and attempted to strut over to us. His alcohol intake, however, made his strut appear more like a bad dance move.

"Missed that pretty face around here," Ryan said teasingly as he motioned for Leann to move over so he could take her spot beside me.

"I see how it is. You only come around when Saw's here. No love for me." He leaned toward me and leered. I could smell the beer on his breath, and I knew he'd already consumed one too many. This was a typical Ryan reaction to drinking. He flirted with everyone.

"This is a couple's kind of place, and my other half isn't around." I forced the smile on my lips to stay in place. He slipped his arm around my waist and pulled me up against his side.

"I can fix that for ya, sweetheart. I'll ditch the bitch I'm with if you promise to follow me out into those woods."

I glanced over at Leann for assistance, and all I got was a wild-eyed panicked expression. She began scanning the crowd. I knew she was searching for Noah to come to the rescue.

"Um, that's okay, Ryan," I said, and started to stand up. I wasn't fast enough, because both his hands were on my waist, pulling me onto his lap before I could get away. My heart was racing, and I fought the urge to scream.

"Let her go, Ryan. If Sawyer hears about this, he'll kill you." Leann's demand went ignored. Ryan chuckled and ran his hand up my leg. I slapped it away and struggled to stand up again.

"Sawyer's not here," he said, holding me firmly in place.

"Ryan, man, let her go," Kyle Jacobson called out as he jogged over toward us. Luckily, Ryan's loud voice had caught Kyle's attention. He reached out to take my hand and pull me up.

Ryan laughed. "I was just having some fun. She's the only piece of hot ass I haven't gotten any of in this town. Sawyer keeps her all to himself."

Kyle squeezed my hand. "The only ass you need to be worried about is your own. Once Sawyer hears about this, he's gonna beat the shit outta ya."

Ryan stood up and stumbled a little bit, proving just how much he'd had to drink. "Aw, I was just having a little fun. No harm down. All that sweet untouched beauty is still in place. Go on now and run along, little preacher's daughter," Ryan called out as I scrambled back toward Leann's car. I didn't check to see if she was following me. I just knew I had to get away.

I reached her car and jerked on the handle, only to find it locked. The tears I'd been holding back trickled down my face. I took a deep breath, letting the rest of the tears free. Why Ryan's behavior bothered me so much I wasn't sure. It wasn't like he'd actually hurt me. My stomach rolled, and I pressed both my hands against it, praying I didn't get sick. Sawyer had been my shield for so long, I didn't know how to react to situations like that one. I hated being so naive.

The bad Ashton would've known what to do. I let out

a sob and laid my forehead against the cool window of the car door. Two arms slipped around my waist, and I started to scream until the smell of Irish Spring soap met my nose.

"It's me. You're safe." At the sound of Beau's voice, I let out a sob and spun around to throw myself into his arms.

"I'm sorry I wasn't there. I came too late. But I swear to you, Ryan Mason won't ever come near you again." His words caused me to cry harder, and I clung to his shirt, burying my head in his chest.

"Shh, it's okay, Ash. Let me get you in the truck before any-one comes searching for either of us," he whispered in my ear. I let him lead me to his truck and put me inside.

"I told Leanne I'd take care of you," he said as he got into the truck. I wiped my face and nodded.

"Thank you. I told her coming here was a bad idea. I've never been without Sawyer." I tried to make my voice sound light, but I failed.

Beau cranked the truck, then leaned over and opened the glove compartment. It was then I noticed the blood covering his knuckles. Gasping, I reached for his hand.

"Oh my God."

A low chuckle vibrated from his chest as he took the rag he'd pulled out of the glove compartment and wiped the blood off his hand.

"It isn't my blood, Ash," he reassured me. Slowly I released his wrist and let him finish cleaning off what I assumed was Ryan's blood.

"Like I said, Ryan won't come near you again."

I nodded, not sure what I was supposed to say. I'd never had anybody beat someone up for me before. It was a strange feeling. The warmth rushing over me as I watched Beau's slightly scratched knuckles come clean was surprising. Apparently, I liked the idea of him smashing in Ryan's face.

"I'm sorry I haven't called." I tore my eyes off Beau's hand to gaze up into his eyes. The worried expression in them tugged at my heart.

"You don't have to apologize. I have no reason to expect you to call me. I just hope my being at your place didn't cause problems for you and Nicole." Okay, that was a lie, but he didn't know it.

"Doesn't matter what she says. I make my own decisions."

I wanted to ask him what he meant by that comment, but I didn't say anything.

"Do you want to go home now?" he asked

Not if I could stay with him, but the truth would only cause us more problems.

"Um, well, I don't have anywhere else to go."

Beau glanced over at me and a mischievous grin tilted the corner of his lips. I couldn't help but smile back at him.

"What about a game of pool?"

"Pool?"

"Yes, pool. There's a little place outside the city limits where I go to get away and shoot pool."

I nodded slowly before admitting, "I don't know how to play pool."

He smirked. "I was hoping you'd say that."

Beau pulled into the small, graveled parking lot of a bar. Motorcycles, beat-up old trucks, and a few older model sports cars filled the limited space. I glanced over a Beau. "This is a bar."

He chuckled and leaned over me to open the truck door. "Yes, princess, it is. Beer and pool go together. Where'd you think we were going?"

This sounded like a bad idea. Actually, I knew it was a bad idea. I hesitated as Beau got out of the truck. He walked around and stopped at my door, holding out his hand.

"Come on, Ash. I promise no one in here will bite you." I swallowed nervously and slipped my hand into his. I wanted to live a little, and this was definitely living a little.

"Let's do this," I said, smiling up at him. He squeezed my hand before leading me inside.

As we stepped inside, a band was playing a really bad version of "Sweet Home Alabama" on a small, makeshift stage. Cigarette smoke, beer, and cheap perfume combined to make an unpleasant smell. I fought the urge to cover my nose. Greasy-looking men, with stomachs that hung over their jeans, tattoos on their arms, and trashy-looking women perched on their laps or draped against them as they danced, littered the place. Beau let go of my hand and slipped his arm around my waist.

He bent his head down and whispered, "I need to show possessiveness in here in order to keep the others away from you."

I had no complaints, so I nodded and pressed up against him. "Um, aren't they going to kick us out? We're underage."

Beau chuckled and led me over to an empty pool table.

"Nope." He glanced over at the bar and gave someone a little nod, then grabbed two pool sticks and handed one to me.

"Now it's time I taught you how to play some pool."

The wicked gleam in his eyes made me want to agree to anything he asked.

"Beau, what're ya doin' bringing the preacher's daughter here?" asked a lady with long, black hair and barely any clothes on as she sat a beer down in front of him. She turned her gaze my way, and I saw familiar hazel eyes staring at me with concern. This was Honey Vincent, Beau's mother. I'd seen glimpses of her on rare occasions when she came to pick Beau up from Sawyer's. But I'd never actually spoken to her. She was gorgeous, even with the thick makeup and cheap clothing.

"Mama, you remember Ashton," Beau said before taking a

swig of his beer. I smiled at her even though she was studying me like I was a strange animal at the zoo. "Hello, Ms. Vincent. It's nice to see you again."

She tilted her head and a lock of long dark hair fell over her shoulder. "Since when did Sawyer's sweet little girlfriend start slumming it at the bar?" I tensed and glanced over at Beau.

"Mama, that's enough. Ashton and I are friends. We've been for most of our life. I'm keeping her company while Sawyer's out of town." Honey looked me up and down before turning back to Beau and shaking her head.

"If that's what you want to tell yourself, son, but I ain't stupid, and for her sake I hope she ain't either." Then she touched Beau's cheek with her hand and turned to walk back to the bar.

"Bring Ash a Coke," he called out after her. She raised her hand in the air and wiggled her deep red fingernails as a way of acknowledgment.

"Sorry about her, but she isn't a big fan of Sawyer's parents, so anything connected to them is instantly questionable. She'll warm up to you after she gets to know you."

I wasn't sure I was brave enough to get to know Honey Vincent. She reminded me of an adult version of Nicole. Instead of sharing those thoughts, I just nodded. Beau grinned and walked over to stand behind me.

"Now for your first lesson in pool. We'll do a few practice rounds before we actually play." Beau put his stick down and nodded toward the one in my hand. "You're going to hit the white ball into the other balls and break them," he explained.

I took the stick, bent over the table, and tried to remember all the times I'd watched people play pool on television. Before I could think too hard, Beau's warm body closed in behind me. His hand covered mine, making me light-headed. It took me a second to remember to breathe.

"This is the part I've been looking forward to," he murmured in my ear as he adjusted my hands on the stick. The heat from his body made me want to snuggle up against him. I tried to stay focused, but I could feel his warm breath on my ear, and his hip was touching my butt. His chest barely grazed my back.

"You're shivering, Ash," he whispered.

I didn't know how to respond. I couldn't blame the shivering on being cold. I was inside an overly warm bar in the middle of the summer.

"Now you're ready to make the shot." His voice sent chills over my body, and I nodded, afraid that if I gazed up at him, I'd throw myself in his arms. Instead I let him guide me into making the shot. Colorful balls rolled all over the table, but I couldn't seem to concentrate.

"Good job. We've got to decide which ball we want to sink, then set up your next shot."

I closed my eyes and took a steadying breath as he stood up

and left the close proximity of my body. I straightened, praying my knees wouldn't buckle beneath me.

Beau's gaze made my cheeks flush. A pleased grin touched his lips, and I suddenly wanted to know how those lips would feel pressed against mine. I couldn't take my eyes off them. Even when his smile vanished, I continued to stare at his mouth.

"You're gonna have to stop doing that, Ash," Beau whispered huskily, and closed the space between us. His body was suddenly pressed against mine. I managed to shake my fascination with his lips and gaze up into his eyes. He was staring down at me with a hungry gleam I wasn't accustomed to seeing. But I liked it. I liked it a lot.

"Ash, I'm trying real hard to be good. Good isn't my thing, but Sawyer's important to me. Please remember I've got my limits, and you studying my mouth like you want a taste is pushing me dangerously close to the edge of those limits."

Swallowing nervously, I nodded. I couldn't speak just yet because I was pretty sure I'd ask him to follow through with whatever he might be considering.

He let out a frustrated sigh, then turned me around to face the pool table.

"Now back to business. Looks like the solids have the best setup, so you can be solids and I'll take stripes. Your red ball is in the best spot. It's almost at the corner pocket over there, and your white ball is very close to it. So go back in position."

I managed to stay focused on what he was telling me, until, once again, he moved in behind me to correct the way I was holding the stick.

"Slow and easy, Ash."

I took a deep, steadying breath and hit the white ball. It rolled straight for the red ball and the red ball sank into the hole.

"I did it!" I squealed, and twirled around to throw my arms around Beau's neck. It wasn't until his arms wrapped around me and I got a very enticing whiff of his soap smell that I realized this hadn't been a wise move.

"Yes, you did," he said, chuckling, then kissed the top of my head. I forced myself to drop my hands and step back away from him.

"Okay, now which one do I hit?" I asked, smiling up at him like my heart wasn't racing in my chest from having him hold me.

He studied the table and nodded. "The blue one is in a good spot."

Two games later I managed to get the hang of it. Watching Beau play pool proved to be extremely entertaining. I'd never realized a guy leaning over a pool table could be sexy, but after watching Beau, I'd decided that this was a very sexy game. Aside from when he bent his tall, muscular body over a table, a small frown line appearing between his eyes as he concentrated, making me want to kiss it. He also made the whole leaning a hip on the table, while he waited on me to take a shot, appear as if he were modeling for a magazine.

"I can't decide if I like the Ash who needed my assistance or the Ash who has it under control better. One way, I get to touch you and get away with it. But the other way, I get to watch you lean over the table. I've got to tell you that it's one really hot look for you."

I kept my gaze on the table instead of meeting his eyes. Hearing him call me hot made me want to grin like an idiot. I didn't want him to get a chance to see my reaction to his words.

"It's getting late. You ready to head out?" Beau asked.

I walked over to him and handed him the pool stick.

"Probably should go," I replied.

He nodded and took the sticks and put them away. I stared down at the only beer he'd drank for the night, and I realized he was being careful for my sake.

"I see you eyeing the beer, and if you want to check, it's still half full."

Smiling, I shook my head. "I believe you."

He reached for my hand and led me toward the exit.

"See ya, Mom," he called as we passed his mother, who was carrying a tray full of beer-filled mugs.

Her gaze flicked from him to me. She smirked, reminding me of Beau.

"All right, y'all, be careful on the way home," she replied.

I hadn't expected that sort of reply from Honey Vincent. She didn't appear to be the type of mother who told you to be careful, especially since she served beer to her son.

Beau's hand slipped around my waist and pulled me up against him again.

"You're getting checked out by some drunk men. I'm just keeping them away," he said quietly as we walked outside. Telling him I didn't mind being pressed up against his side didn't seem like a good idea, so I kept my mouth shut.

Once we were buckled in, I studied the rundown bar where I'd just spent the last couple of hours. It wasn't nearly as scary as I'd thought a bar would be. After we'd started playing pool, I'd forgotten all about everyone else in the place. Beau pulled his truck out onto the two-lane road that led back into town. The lights from the parking lot faded in the distance as we drove farther away from the bar and closer to my house. I wasn't ready to go home yet. Tonight had been the most fun I'd ever had on a date. Even if it wasn't a date, really. I laughed when I was with Beau much more than I ever did any other time. I'd forgotten how much fun Beau was. Maybe that was why I had always chosen to sneak off with him when I was a kid. Sawyer was always there keeping us in line, and I loved him. But Beau always led to excitement.

"Thanks for tonight. I really had fun."

"I could tell. I liked watching you have fun. You're incredible when you let that wall down around yourself."

"Wall?" I asked, turning to face him.

He didn't say anything at first. But I kept my eyes fixed on him, waiting.

"Your perfect wall. The one you keep up for the world to see. The one you use to hide the girl I know underneath. The girl who wants to laugh and have fun. Perfect isn't fun, Ash."

I let the bad girl out with Beau because I knew he wouldn't shun her or reprimand her. He knew a part of me I didn't show anyone else. Sure, Grana always encouraged me to make my own decisions and embrace the real me, but I still kept the truly bad side of me hidden, even from her. I wanted to argue with him and throw my wall up to block out his seeing inside, but I couldn't. I needed him to let me be me. No one other than Grana ever let me stretch and spread my wings. Beau had always been the only other person to accept me as I am.

I nodded and fixed my eyes back on the road in front of us.

"I can't be that girl all the time. My parents, Sawyer, the people in this town, they all expect the good girl. I can't let them see this side of me. But it feels so good to let her loose. If only for a little while. So thank you."

I didn't glance back to see his reaction, but I didn't need to. His hand reached for mine, and he held it. No words were needed because he understood.

Chapter 6

ASHTON

I woke up to find my mother sitting on the edge of my bed. Even though my vision was still blurry from sleep, it was hard to miss her bloodshot eyes and the dark circles underneath them.

"Mom," I asked, wanting to reach for her and comfort her. The little girl inside me was terrified to see my mom so obviously upset.

"Good morning, sweetheart. I'm sorry if I woke you, but I wanted to talk to you before Dad got back home."

Immediately my stomach dropped.

"Ashton, honey, Grana passed away."

All other thoughts left my mind.

"What?"

Mom let out a small sob and reached for one of my hands. Her gentle squeeze didn't comfort me.

"Last night Grana went to sleep. When Dad got there this morning to fix her water heater, before he went to the church, he found her in bed. It was a heart attack."

I shook my head, not believing what my mother was saying. I had to still be dreaming. This couldn't be happening. We had plans. Grana and I. There were so many things we still had to do.

"Sweetie, I know you were close to Grana. This is hard on all of us, but I know it's hardest on you. It's okay to cry. I'm here and I'll hold you."

I'd never thought about Grana dying. She was a fixture in my life. My escape from the world I lived in daily. She understood me in a way my parents never had. Grana never expected me to be perfect like my parents and Sawyer did. Being with her was freeing. It was like, like when I was with Beau. I could be myself and I knew she loved me. An emptiness settled inside me as tears rolled down my face. I still needed her. How could she be gone? I'd just been to see her. She'd just told me how no one could be as perfect with Beau without his shirt on. We'd laughed together. She'd just had a pedicure. How could she be dead? She wasn't ready to die. Her toes had been hot pink. She was ready for some fun. We had plans to go to the movies together.

My mother's arms came around me, pulling me into her

embrace. All my life I'd found comfort in her arms, but now I only felt numb. My Grana wouldn't be there for my wedding day. We'd never take that cruise together or go scuba diving in the Bahamas. She wouldn't be there to make sugar cookies for my kids one day. Where would I find an escape from the pressure of my life? How could I live without her?

Ashton,

Again, sorry for the long delays in e-mails. After a full day of hiking, I crash when we get back to the cabin. I'm fighting off exhaustion so I can write you. Today Cade and I took a special trail that my mom and sister didn't want to try. So Dad stayed with them. It was pretty steep in areas. It was great. The view we finally came to was amazing, and Cade got to see his first black bear. I think he took a dozen pictures of it.

Hang in there. Your boredom is almost halfway over. I'll be home in twenty days.

Love ya,

Sawyer

Sawyer,

Hey . . .

I didn't want to tell a computer screen that my Grana had died. I couldn't tell him about washing the car with Beau and playing pool in a bar. My vision was blurred from crying, and typing on a computer was the last thing I wanted to do. I erased my response, grabbed my purse, and headed for my car. I could lie to myself and say I didn't know where I was going, that I just needed to get away and drive. But I knew deep down exactly where I was headed.

I parked my Jetta out by Mr. Jackson's barn. Beau hadn't been home, but his mother had taken one look at my stricken face and told me where I could find him.

I heard the tractor before I saw it. My feet started walking toward the sound. I needed someone to help me forget the awful truth. I didn't need a stupid e-mail telling me about waterfalls and bears. I needed someone here, and the first person that came to my mind was Beau. He wouldn't tell me everything would be okay. He wouldn't try to appease me like a child. I needed him.

The minute he saw me walking across the field, the tractor stopped. His eyes locked on me and I started to run. I could feel the wetness on my face from my tears as I ran toward him. He jumped down just before I reached him.

Beau caught me as I flung myself into his arms. The silent tears turned into loud sobs for the first time since my mother had told me Grana was gone. He didn't ask. I'd known he wouldn't. He would wait until I was ready.

BEAU

I pulled Ashton onto my lap as I sat down under an old oak tree. Her arms tightened around my neck as she sobbed pitifully against my chest. I was scared to ask what was wrong. Instead I held her and waited. My chest ached so bad with each sob that it was difficult to take deep breaths. Sitting here and waiting on her to calm down enough to tell me who I needed to go beat the shit out of for making her cry wasn't easy. A sob shook her body, and I cradled her tighter against me. My heart had a spasm with each tremble of her body. Even when we were kids, I didn't like to see her upset. The one time a kid had hurt her feelings on the playground, I'd reacted by shoving the kid's face in the dirt. It had gotten me two days suspension, but it'd been worth it. No one bothered her again. They knew better.

Her sobs slowly began to ease to soft little whimpers. I gazed down at her as she lifted her head from my sweaty chest. Her big green eyes stared up at me, and the tightness in my chest throbbed. If someone had hurt her, I would kill them. If Sawyer was the cause of this, I would take him down. Cousin or not, no one was allowed to make Ashton cry.

"My Grana had a heart attack last night. She's gone," she whispered.

I hadn't expected that.

"I'm sorry, baby."

"Just hold me please," she replied.

I'd hold her forever if I could.

I gently moved the hair stuck to her tear-soaked face back and tucked it behind her ears. She glanced down and tensed as she finally noticed my lack of a shirt. My chest was now soaked with not only sweat but her tears. I started to say something, but the words got stuck in my throat as her hand moved up to my chest and she began softly wiping the droplets of moisture off me. I stopped breathing. I knew it was wrong to let her do this, but I couldn't bring myself to care. She shifted in my lap until she was straddling me. I let my hands fall to her waist as she continued touching my chest. My heart started slamming against my ribs so hard I knew she had to feel it. I needed to stop this.

"Beau," she said.

I tore my eyes away from her hands on my chest and gazed up at her face. There was a question in her eyes. I could see it.

"Yes." I managed a strangled reply.

Her hands left me, and I started to take a deep breath to ease my burning, oxygen-deprived lungs when I realized why she'd stopped driving me crazy with her innocent caresses. That deep breath lodged in my throat as her top came off. Without taking her eyes off me, she dropped the little tank top onto the grass beside her. I had thought nothing could be sexier than Ashton in a bikini; I'd been so wrong. Ashton in a lacy white bra was by far the sexiest thing I'd ever seen.

"Ash, baby, what're you doing?" I asked in a hoarse whisper. I tried forcing myself to look up at her face and gauge what she was thinking, but I couldn't take my eyes off her boobs.

"Touch me," she whispered. The fact she was Sawyer's girl no longer seemed to matter. I couldn't tell her no. Hell, I couldn't tell myself no.

I traced a line from her collarbone to the top of her cleavage. She gasped loudly and sank down in my lap, applying pressure to my cock. She was going to send me into a crazed frenzy if she kept it up. As if she could read my thoughts, she seemed to test me as she wiggled her ass in my lap.

"Ah, damn," I moaned before grabbing her face and pulling her mouth to mine.

The moment my mouth touched hers, my world started spinning beneath me. I couldn't get enough. I had her bra off and my hands full within seconds. The loud moan of pleasure that escaped from her mouth almost sent me over the edge.

I'd lost my virginity at the age of thirteen and there had been many girls since then, but nothing had prepared me for this feeling. Ashton wrapped her arms around my neck and pressed her bare chest up against mine, causing me to shudder for the first time in my life. I kissed a trail from her mouth to her ear then down her neck. I'd crossed the line kissing her and touching her. I needed to stop this.

"Please, Beau," she pleaded, and sat up on her knees, presenting her tight, pink nipples to my incredibly eager mouth.

I was weak, and more turned on than I'd been in my entire life.

More than an hour later I held her as she sat curled up in my lap. I was waiting on the horror of what I'd done to wash over me, but having Ashton in my arms wasn't helping me work up the remorse I should be feeling. Instead I finally felt alive.

ASHTON

I opened my car door and turned to peek back at Beau. My heart fluttered wildly at the sight of him. I'd wanted to go all the way, but he'd stopped us. A smile tugged at my lips; I knew he hadn't stopped me because it was wrong. Or because he didn't want to. He had stopped only because we'd had no protection. Beau had been as deliriously turned on as I'd been. He'd looked at me with those beautiful hazel eyes, no longer hiding his feelings.

"Can you get out tonight?" he asked me as he stepped toward me just close enough to touch my waist. The skin where his hand grazed tingled with anticipation.

"Yes, it'll be late, though. I've got to go to Grana's. People will be bringing food and all that stuff. I'll need to see you to cheer me up. Make me forget." I'd crawl out my window for him if I had to.

He stepped closer, and I watched as he lowered his mouth to mine. Just like before, the earth fell out from under me with the touch of his lips. I clung to his shoulders, afraid I'd fall if he let me go. He broke the kiss and moved his mouth to my ear. I shivered and pressed closer to him.

"Text me when you're ready, and I'll meet you at the park behind your house," he whispered, then stepped back.

I grabbed the door for support before nodding and getting into my car.

"Where did you run off to last night?" Leann whispered as she plopped down on the step beside me.

I'd decided to hide out on the stairs once Grana's house was filled to capacity with people. They were suffocating me. Leann was here with her mother, and I appreciated it, but I wasn't in the mood to talk. I studied her expression to see if she had any idea Beau had taken me to play pool before taking me home. I'd texted her to let her know he was driving me home because I had a headache, and I'd left it at that.

"Beau offered to take me home, so I went. I wasn't in the mood to hang out after the incident with Ryan."

She leaned over closer to me, bumping her shoulder against mine. "Girl, you should've seen the bloody mess Beau made of Ryan's face. He beat the crap out of him. It was hot."

I rolled my eyes at her words, hiding the secret thrill I felt over having Beau stand up for me.

"Don't roll your eyes. You have no idea how hot he was beating Ryan's face in. He kept warning him he'd kill him if he even looked in your direction again."

I opened my mouth to respond as the smell of intense old lady perfume wafted over me.

"Ashton, sweetie, I'm so sorry," said Mrs. Murphy, one of the ladies from church who Grana had always said needed to wear more makeup to cover her bags and less perfume because she was polluting the atmosphere. Mrs. Murphy stopped in front of me and held out her hands.

Everyone wanted to hug me, as if a hug was going to make me feel better. Mrs. Murphy's habit of bathing in her cheap perfume caused a headache with close contact. So I patted her hands awkwardly, hoping she didn't grab mine and jerk me up into her arms. I could see the white, used tissue in her grasp, and I wasn't thrilled about having to touch it or have it touch me.

"Thanks, Mrs. Murphy." I replied.

She sniffed and dotted at her eyes with the tissue. "It's just so hard to believe. I mean, she was just at the ladies auxiliary meeting on Monday. It's awful, just awful."

I didn't need this. Why people thought I wanted to hear about the last time they saw Grana was beyond me. I was trying to forget. I wanted to pretend she and I were going to curl up on the swing together when everyone was gone and talk about funny things we saw or someone said. I didn't need to get a play-by-play from everyone here on the last time they saw my Grana alive.

"Thanks, Mrs. Murphy. Ashton is dealing with things the best she can. She appreciates your words, but she isn't up to talking about everything just yet." Leann's words were perfect. Mrs. Murphy gave me one last sad smile and nodded before making her way over to someone who would talk to her.

"Thanks," I said, glancing over at Leann.

She wrapped her arm around my shoulders. "That's what friends are for."

I nodded and laid my head over on her shoulder. I was going to miss her this year at school. I'd never had many girlfriends. I'd grown up with the Vincent boys as my two best friends. I wasn't good with girl friendships. Leann had been my first girlfriend my freshman year. She'd been a sophomore and had taken me under her wing.

"What am I going to do without you this year?"

"You have prince charming. You'll do fine. Besides, I'll be only a phone call away." Tears stung my eyes. I'd lost Grana and I was losing Leann. My world was changing so quickly. I really needed Beau right now. He would make sense of everything. He'd listen to me complain and feel sorry for myself and not try to make me look on the bright side. Wrapped up in his arms was where I wanted to be. Not here with a bunch of people in Grana's house and a kitchen full of casseroles and pies.

"I'm going to a movie with Leann," I said as soon as we walked into our house.

The last of the visitors at Grana's had finally gone, leaving us with more food than we could eat in a year. I placed the sweet potato casserole on the bar and turned to look at my parents.

"You're going to a movie this late?" Dad asked, frowning as he put down several pies he'd carried inside.

"It's a midnight viewing for a vampire movie or something. She doesn't want to go alone, and I need to get my mind off things."

My mom, who appeared better this evening than she had this morning, smiled. She seemed pleased I wasn't planning on crawling into bed to cry. *I wonder how she'd feel if she knew I was planning on crawling into the arms of the town's bad boy to cry instead?* I couldn't worry about what her or Dad thought. Staying here, looking into my dad's sad eyes and at my mother's tentative smile, would only cause me more pain. When I was with Beau, I could forget for a little while.

"Good. Go out and have some fun. You've been spending too much time alone since Sawyer left. It isn't good to be alone all the time," Mom encouraged. Dad hadn't seemed to be able to say much today. Looking at him caused the pain in my chest to reopen. I glanced back at Mom.

"I know. I just needed to adjust to Sawyer being gone. I hadn't realized how much time I spent with him until he wasn't here."

Mom liked my response. She loved Sawyer, but she always reminded me how getting too serious this young wasn't a good idea. I still had college ahead of me. The guilt of what I was doing with Beau eased even more when I looked at my mom's smile. I was lying to her about who I was with and what I was doing, but in a roundabout way I was doing what she wanted.

Normally, this was when my dad would tell me to be careful and be home by eleven. Tonight he remained silent, lost in his own world of pain. I gave them one last smile and headed for the door.

Chapter 7

ASHTON

I walked the short trail from my house to the park. I didn't want to leave my car sitting in the parking lot for everyone to see. It wouldn't take much for them to realize that Beau had been parked there earlier and now my empty car was in its place. No one expected the preacher's daughter to sin, but they sure would love to catch me at it. Not that this was a sin, exactly. Well, lying to my parents was, but Beau was Sawyer's cousin and my . . . friend. I was pretty sure some of the places Beau had touched me and kissed me this afternoon fell into the sin category, but I couldn't bring myself to care. By the time I reached the park, I'd almost convinced myself of our innocence.

The park was deserted except for the beat-up Chevy truck. I ran to the passenger's side and jumped in before someone could drive up and catch me. Beau was smiling at me; my heartbeat picked up its pace.

"I really like it when you wear sundresses," he said before cranking up the truck and pulling out onto the road. I glanced down at the short hem on the baby blue sundress I'd picked out, and a tingle of anticipation ran through me.

"I'm not going back through town. Come over here," he said, patting the spot beside him. I scooted over as close as I could without my legs touching the stick shift.

"That's not close enough. Straddle it," he said. I glanced over at him, and he took his eyes off the road for just a moment to meet my gaze. My heart did a little fluttery thing against my chest. I moved a leg over the stick shift and scooted over until my thigh was up against his. As his hand rested on the stick shift between my knees, I was suddenly light-headed.

"How late do I get to keep you tonight?" he asked, breaking into my thoughts.

"Oh, um, they didn't say, but then, I don't normally go out this late. I told them I was going to a midnight movie."

He shifted gears then rested his hand on my thigh. I was beginning to understand why he liked sundresses.

"Good, we've got time to go to the bay," he replied.

I hadn't been to the bay in years. Sawyer never wanted to drive out that way. He said the water was nasty, but I always thought it was beautiful.

"I figured it would be best if we didn't hang out around here."

I nodded because I understood his meaning. He didn't seem bothered by the fact he was doing things with his cousin's girlfriend that he shouldn't be. The thought reminded me of the image I'd had of Beau the past few years. He played games to his advantage. The sexy rebel who took what he wanted. Except that image no longer seemed accurate. He'd held me today without question as I cried and slobbered all over him. He'd stopped working to comfort me. Someone with selfish motives wouldn't do that. Besides, if what we were doing meant he had a black heart, then I had one too.

"You're frowning. What's going through your head?" he asked.

I thought about lying to him, since I was becoming a regular old liar, but I couldn't lie to him, too. This was something I needed to talk about before . . . well, before we went all the way.

"How I know I'm doing something wrong and I feel guilty, but neither of those things matters enough to make me stop."

Beau's hand left my thigh and returned to the stick shift. I studied his large, tanned hand and wondered how it was fair for someone to be given all perfect body parts. His grip on the stick was so tight, the tanned color of his skin had paled. I wanted to reach out and soothe him, make the tension go away, but we had to talk about this. He didn't say anything else or make a move to touch me. A sick knot of dread settled in my stomach as I waited to see if he was going to turn around and take me back.

I'd reminded him of how wrong what we were doing was and he wasn't dealing with it well. He loved Sawyer, and I'd never imagined he'd do something like this to his cousin. I wasn't any better. I was supposed to love Sawyer too and I did, but not the way I should. As the silence stretched on, I waited for Beau to turn the truck around and take me back to the park, but he kept heading toward the bay. After a few minutes, when I was sure he wasn't going to turn around, I relaxed and waited.

Beau pulled onto a dirt road, and through the overgrown grass and weeds I could see a clearing ahead. It was complete with a pier. Beau turned his truck and backed it up so the rear bumper was facing the water.

"Where are we?" I asked

"A piece of property a friend of mine owns. He bought it to build on when he gets out of college," he replied, and reached to open the door.

I started to scoot over so I could get out on the other side, when his hand touched my leg, causing me to tremble before I glanced back at him.

"Wait here. I'm going to fix it up back there, then get you and carry you back. The grass is high and there could be snakes in it."

I nodded and watched as he jumped down into the tall grass. The snakes bothered me some, but the idea of him carrying me was causing other ideas to form in my head, keeping me occupied while I waited. Within minutes he was back, standing outside the open truck door. He crooked his finger for me to come to him. I slid over until I was close enough for him to grab me under my legs and carry me. The moment he picked me up, I suddenly worried I might be too heavy. I tried not to dwell on my weight, but I didn't normally have guys picking me up and carrying me around. Luckily, my weight didn't seem to be an issue as he carried me around the back of the truck and lifted me onto its bed with ease.

He'd spread out several quilts and a couple of pillows. A cooler was in the far corner. I crawled to the middle and sat down. Beau stood at the tailgate, watching me. The shadows from the moonlight shaded his eyes, so I couldn't be sure what he was thinking.

"Are you coming?" I asked, almost scared of his answer.

"Yeah, I got a little sidetracked by the view," he replied.

A shiver of anticipation ran through me as he crawled onto the truck bed. Kneeling in front of me, he reached out to take my right foot and lay it against his jean-clad thigh. Fascinated, I watched him as he undid my sandal and placed it beside the cooler. He placed my foot back down on the blanket then reached for my left foot, and with the same slow careful attention, he removed my other sandal. Once both my feet were bare, he lifted his gaze to meet mine.

A small smile tugged at the corner of his lips. "I like your pink toenails," he replied, glancing back down at my feet. My silly heart thumped wildly in my chest, and I let out a nervous laugh.

"It's cotton candy. The color is, I mean." I couldn't even form coherent sentences.

"I like cotton candy. Those toes of yours just may be sweeter, though."

As he moved to sit down beside me, his warm hand squeezed my foot closest to him. Neither of us spoke as we stared out over the still water. I'd never been so nervous in my life.

Beau shifted beside me and then lay back on the pillows behind us. I turned slightly to peer down at him. Did he want me to lie down too? Tucking one arm behind his head and stretching the other out beside him, Beau grinned up at me as if he could read my mind.

"Come here," he said.

I quickly scooted over and curled up next to him him, resting my head on his chest. There was a peace in his arms I'd never experienced with Sawyer. It was as if I'd come home after years of searching.

"I love Sawyer, Ash," Beau said quietly into the night. He sounded as if he were trying to convince me of this. "My whole life, I've never envied anything of his. Not his father. Not his mother. Not his money. Not his athletic abilities." He stopped and took a ragged breath.

My heart ached for him. I squeezed my hand, which was resting on his stomach, into a fist to keep from reaching up and soothing him like a child.

"Until the day I watched from across the football field as he picked you up and kissed you on the mouth," he continued. "It wasn't your first kiss. I might have just been fourteen years old, but I could tell I'd somehow been left out of a secret. I wanted to plant my fist in his face and rip you out of his arms. As I took a step toward him, your eyes met mine and I saw the silent pleading for forgiveness or acceptance. I wasn't sure which. All I knew then was that you were Sawyer's. My best friend was gone. I envied him and hated him for the first time that day. He'd finally won the one prize I'd thought was mine."

I closed my eyes against the tears threatening to spill down my cheeks. I wanted to tell him how I'd never felt faint when Sawyer kissed me or how the earth didn't move under his touch. Instead I stayed silent, knowing I couldn't. Even though it was Beau I wanted, I knew I could never have him. These last two weeks were all we had. Sawyer would come home and I would be with him again. There was no other option.

I turned over and propped myself up on my elbow until I was staring down into his somber eyes. I could feel his heart beating fast underneath my hand.

"You were my best friend, Beau. You never treated me or looked at me any way but as a friend. Once I started to change and we all began to notice the opposite sex, you never seemed to care that I was a girl. Sawyer did. Maybe because he hadn't been my partner in crime. Maybe because the connection I had with him hadn't been the same as the one I had had with you. But he saw me as a girl. I think deep down I'd been waiting on you, but when he kissed me, I knew it would never be you. I wasn't the one for you."

Beau reached up and cupped the side of my face with his hand.

"I was very aware that you were a girl, Ash. I was just scared, because the one person in the world who knew every secret I'd ever had also happened to be the most beautiful girl I'd ever known. My feelings for you were scary as hell."

I leaned down and kissed the frown between his brows.

"Right now. Right here. I'm yours. Not Sawyer's. He isn't who I want. Right now all I want is you." I chose my words carefully so we'd both understand my meaning.

He took my waist and shifted his body so I was completely on top of him. I lowered my mouth to his and sighed as his hands found the hem of my dress and the warm pressure of his palms ran up my thighs.

Tonight I would give myself to Beau because I wanted to. He was the town's bad boy and I was the preacher's daughter. It wasn't supposed to happen this way.

"Ash, I want you. Bad, very, very bad. But you deserve better than this."

I bent back down over him and kissed him again before pulling back enough to whisper, "It doesn't get any better than this, Beau."

His hands cupped my bottom and shifted me so I could feel the pressure of his obvious arousal against the warmth between my thighs.

"Please, Beau," I cried out, not sure what I was begging for but knowing I needed more. His hands gripped my waist.

"Hold on to me, baby. I'm going to take care of you." The raspy need in his voice only made me more desperate.

Chapter 8

BEAU

Today I was supposed to cut three different lawns, but I'd just called and rescheduled all of them moments before Ashton came running out of the woods and toward my truck. Last night had changed everything for me. I needed to tell her exactly how I felt, but I couldn't do it right then. I didn't want to have that conversation yet. I just wanted to enjoy being with her. We were going to spend the day at the beach and blend in with all the tourists. Hanging out together in town wasn't an option. At least, not until Sawyer came home and I talked with him. I couldn't let her go. Not now. This one time in my life, I wasn't going to sit back and watch Sawyer have it all. I needed Ashton. I loved her in a way I knew my cousin never could.

She opened the passenger door and climbed inside. God help me. She had on a pair of tiny shorts and an even tinier top, giving me a peek at her belly button. The beach was a forty-five minute drive, and she was going to make me crazy, dressed like that.

"Good morning," she said, smiling as she slid over beside me and straddled the stick shift. All worries of Sawyer fled my mind.

"Good morning, beautiful," I replied, and leaned over to kiss her. She immediately sighed and moved closer to me, running her fingers through my hair. It took all my self-control to pull back.

"Don't you want to get out of here first?" I asked.

She pouted as if I'd just taken away her favorite toy and sat back, crossing her arms over her chest.

"How're you feeling today?" I asked, pulling out onto the road. Her dimple winked at me. It took extreme willpower to keep driving and not pull over so I could kiss that sweet spot.

"I'm fine. . . . I mean, better than fine. I'm—" She paused, and I glanced down to see her cheeks flush a pretty, bright pink. I couldn't keep from chuckling at the innocent blush on her face. Reaching down, I gently pulled one of the small hands she was wringing nervously in her lap and threaded my fingers through hers while the first stirrings of possessiveness came over me.

"Are you sore?" I asked. I'd heard virgins were normally sore afterward, but Ashton had been the first virgin I'd ever been with.

She started to shake her head, but then her blush deepened. "Maybe a little."

"I'm sorry," I replied, feeling a tug of protectiveness to go with the healthy heaping of possessiveness rearing up inside me. She was turning my insides into a war zone.

She gazed up at me and smiled shyly. "I'm not."

God, I loved her. She wrapped her arms around mine and laid her head on my shoulder. It was one of the few times I hated my stick shift. I'd prefer to remain just like this without having to move my arm.

"Tell me you put on sunblock," I said, glancing down at her lightly tanned skin. The sun on the beach was intense for even the best tanner. She giggled and nodded her head. All was right with the world. Once I pulled out onto the highway, heading south, I tucked my hand between her thighs and enjoyed the ride.

Normally, I didn't like the tourist-covered beaches. But that day was different. I didn't mind the screaming kids flipping sand in my face as they scampered along the sand or the obnoxious sun-burned northerners who feed the damn seagulls. Ashton made everything better.

The sun was scorching hot, and although Ashton was content to bask in the heat, I kept pulling her into the waves with me. Watching her laugh and play as we dove into the oncoming waves made it feel as if our years apart had just disappeared. There was then and now. The lost time in between was erased. Being with her made me feel complete. She'd always been the one to hold me together when my world crumbled around me.

"Oh my God. There's a jellyfish!" Her shriek was followed by a humorous attempt at running through the rough water toward the sandy beach. I bit back my laughter and followed her. I didn't doubt there was a jellyfish. It was time for them, but seeing her wide eyes and panicked expression was just so cute; it was funny.

ASHTON

"I always knew you would be irresistible once you stopped acting like someone you're not," Beau whispered in my ear as he wrapped his arms around me.

I was still panting from running through the crashing waves. I let out a breathless chuckle and laid my head back against his hard chest.

"It isn't easy hiding the bad girl inside me from the only person who knows she exists," I replied. Beau's arms tightened around me, and his breath was on my neck as he rested his chin on my shoulder.

"No. I never saw a bad girl. You're not bad, Ash. You've just been pretending to be someone else for so long, just to make your parents, and then Sawyer, happy. The girl you really are is amazing. You're kind, yet you've got spunk. You're brilliant, but you never act superior. You're careful, yet you know how to have fun, and you're so incredibly sexy, but you haven't got a clue."

It was hard to see myself the way he described me, but what he said made me wish things were different. I hadn't held back with him at all. When I was with Beau, I didn't pretend to be anything. I was just me. And instead of the bad girl, he saw something desirable. I wanted the world to see me this way too, but I knew that only someone like Beau would find all my faults to be attractive qualities.

"I'm glad you see me that way. I'm not saying I agree, but it makes me happy knowing you don't see the flaws."

Beau tensed behind me for a moment before his arms left me. I could feel his body shift away from mine.

"What's wrong?" I asked, turning around to face him.

He just shook his head. I waited for him to speak, and after a few minutes of silence, he turned his head to study me.

"Why are you with Sawyer?"

This wasn't a question I'd been prepared for. I shook my head. "What do you mean?"

He ran his hand through his hair, closing his eyes as if he

were fighting to keep from saying whatever was on the tip of his tongue.

"You act like someone else with him. Someone you believe would appeal to him. A perfect good girl who follows all the rules. Yet you want to break rules, Ash. You aren't a criminal—you just want to spread your wings a little and enjoy life. But you want him so much, you're willing to deny yourself freedom to be *you* just so you can have him." He stopped talking but kept his pleading gaze on me. I wanted him to stop talking. I didn't want to hear these things. They weren't true. I was a good girl. I was the kind of a girl someone like Sawyer could love.

"I am good," I managed to say through the tightness in my throat. I felt stupid saying the words, especially when just last night I'd lost my virginity in the back of his pickup truck when I should've been home mourning Grana's death. I closed my eyes tightly, trying to force my thoughts of Grana away. I couldn't think about her now. I wasn't ready.

"I didn't say you were bad. You're good, Ash. Were you not listening to me? You have this warped sense of what good is. Wanting to sneak out with your boyfriend and wanting to know you're desirable and wanted by your freaking boyfriend, or leaving a damn buggy in a parking spot, doesn't make you a bad person. It makes you a human."

Tears stung my eyes. I wanted to believe him. I'd lived with guilt for so long because I wanted to do the things I'd been told were wrong. But this was Beau Vincent. He drank too much and did things to girls in public places I'd never done in my life . . . until I'd started spending time with him. Mom had always told me Lucifer was beautiful.

"I'd thought the Ash I knew was completely gone. I mourned her for a long time. Then one day in the lunch room Haley kept coming up to Sawyer and flirting with him right in front of you as if you weren't there. When she turned to walk away, you tripped her. Sawyer didn't see it, but I did." A grin curled up on the corner of his mouth. "When she was splayed out there on the floor, I saw a little smirk touch your lips before you bent down to help her up, apologizing profusely. Until that moment, I'd thought you were lost. I realized my Ash was somewhere under all the polish and politeness. After that day, I started watching you and enjoying the moments when I got a glimpse of the real you slipping out while no one else was paying attention. It's why I said the things to you that I did. I wanted you to react to me. I wanted you to smart off at me. Those moments when you couldn't take it anymore and snapped . . . I lived for those moments."

"You were mean to me because you wanted me to smart off to you?" I asked.

He nodded, then bent down to kiss the tip of my nose.

"You really like my ugly side, don't you, Beau?"

"Nothing about you is ugly. You're just as beautiful inside as you are out, but you don't see it. That's what kills me. Sawyer's my cousin and I'd do anything for him. But he's insane for keeping you up on some damn pedestal. I want the real you. The one that likes shimmying out of a pair of shorts knowing you're driving me wild. The one who runs through the woods to my truck smiling like nothing else matters." He cupped my face with his hand. "The real Ashton Gray is perfect, and I'm crazy in love with her." My gut clenched. I had feelings for Beau. We shared a history together and now we had this summer, but love wasn't supposed to factor into the equation. There was Sawyer standing between us.

Beau's lips found mine and everything else fell away. I didn't care about all the worries and arguments in the back of my head. I just wanted to be me. In his arms I knew I could be.

Chapter 9

ASHTON

Everyone in the town somehow managed to pack themselves into the church to pay their respects to Grana. I hadn't been able to talk myself into going up and looking at her lying there still and pale. They couldn't have done her makeup right. She was a makeup expert and always had herself fixed up pretty. I'd liked knowing I had the prettiest seventy-year-old Grana in the world. When Mom and Dad hadn't wanted me to start wearing makeup yet, even after my begging and pleading with them, Grana spirited me off to stay the weekend with her so she could teach me the technique of "putting on your face," as she called it.

A tear trickled down my cheek, and I reached up to catch it with the Kleenex someone had handed me earlier. So many times I'd stood in the third row with Grana while Dad preached.

We'd write notes back and forth until Mom would cut a sharp warning glare at us. It always made us giggle. Grana would act like we were putting the paper away. In reality she'd just get sneakier. Grana was a lot like Beau; she embraced the bad girl inside me. Thinking of Beau caused another lump to form in my throat. I was starting to depend on him so much. Sawyer would be home soon and everything would change.

"Hey." Beau's deep voice startled me, and I lifted my head to find him standing in front of me. I hadn't expected him to come that night. Besides the fact he never stepped foot in the church except on Easter Sunday and Christmas Eve, I figured he would spend his one night free of me with friends . . . or Nicole.

"Hi," I replied in a hoarse whisper. "I didn't expect you to—" I stopped myself from saying more. He raised both blond eyebrows and tilted his head slightly to the left as he frowned at me. I noticed his short blond hair, which normally had that messy, sexy look, was neatly brushed. My eyes drifted down to his broad shoulders and chest, taking in the pale blue, button-up dress shirt I was positive he'd never worn until then. The shirt was tucked into a pair of tan slacks I'd also never seen him wear. When I lifted my eyes back up to meet his, I smiled for the first time in hours, enjoying his obvious discomfort.

"You dressed up," I said quietly, not wanting to attract attention to us. He shrugged and glanced around as if to see how many more people would notice his attempt at cleaning up.

When his eyes settled back on me, he leaned closer.

"Have you gone up to see her?" His soft whisper caused tears to spring back into my eyes. I shook my head and took a deep breath to keep from breaking down and hurling myself into his arms for comfort in front of the whole town. His warm hand covered mine, and he stepped closer to me as he laced his fingers through mine. Confused, I quickly looked around the church this time to see who was watching us.

"Come on, Ash. You'll regret not going to see her one last time. You need to do this for closure. Trust me." There was a sadness in his eyes as he stared down at me, pleading. "I didn't go see my dad. I regret that. Even to this day."

His admission caused the ache in my chest to throb harder—not just for me and my loss but for the little boy who had lost so much. Somehow he needed me to do this. I let him gently pull me up the aisle toward the open casket holding the one woman I'd always depended on to be there no matter what. We'd talked about my wedding and how she would fix my hair and makeup. We'd planned the colors of the bridesmaid dresses and the bouquets of flowers she would arrange. We'd talked about her making the christening gowns for my children to wear on the day they'd be dedicated in this church. So many plans had been made. So many dreams had been cast as we'd sat on her front porch drinking sweet tea and eating sugar cookies.

The casket was a lovely marble, white with pink lining. She

would love it. She loved pink. The massive splay of white and pink roses that lay over the bottom half of the casket would have delighted her. Those rosebushes she babied and cooed over every spring and summer had been one of her life's joys. I wanted to thank everyone who had sent her the large flower bouquets lining the church walls, especially the ones with roses.

A warm trickle fell from my chin and splashed against my hand. I reached up with my free hand and wiped at my face, but it was pointless. Tears were streaming down my cheeks. I hadn't even realized I was crying.

"I won't leave you, but you need to go on up and say your good-byes. I'll stand right here behind you," Beau whispered from beside me.

Since I'd walked into those familiar double doors, I'd had a tight knot in my chest making it hard to breathe deeply. Then, as I stood there getting ready to say good-bye to the woman I loved so dearly, a peace settled over me. I released the tight grip I had on Beau's hand and stepped forward.

She was smiling. I was glad she was smiling. She smiled a lot. They'd used her makeup. I'd know the color of that ripe raspberry lipstick anywhere. The smell of roses was thick, reminding me even more of the afternoons we'd sat outside her house talking.

"They dressed you in your favorite dress," I whispered as I stared down at her still body. "And they used your makeup.

Although you would have done a better job putting it on. The eye shadow is a little too dark. Whoever put it on apparently doesn't know about the 'less is more' rule."

It was odd talking to her like this. She would have chuckled at the makeup comment. We'd have concocted a scheme to give the morgue beauticians or whoever put makeup on the recently deceased a lesson in the art of "putting on your face." The corners of my mouth lifted.

"Remember when we talked about how we hoped we got to hang around earth long enough to be at our own funerals? Well, in case you convinced God of this idea and you're here somewhere listening"—I paused and swallowed the sob threatening to escape—"if you're here . . . I love you. I miss you. I'm going to think of you every day, and all those plans we had—I'm going to keep them. Just promise you'll be there. Promise you'll convince the big guy to let you come back down to visit."

This time a sob made it past my lips. I covered my mouth and dropped my head as the memories washed over me. Knowing that this was the last time I'd ever see her tore a hole through my chest. A comforting arm wrapped around me and pulled me against his hard chest. Beau didn't say anything to comfort me. He just let me get this last good-bye out the only way I knew how. When the tears subsided and the ache in my chest seemed to ease, I lifted my head to stare up at him.

"I'm a firm believer God doesn't snatch you right up and

haul you off to Heaven. I think he lets you say your good-byes. And your Grana wouldn't have gone anywhere until she got this good-bye in." I let out a small chuckle and nodded. He was right, of course. Even God couldn't have moved her if she wasn't ready.

"Bye, Grana," I whispered one last time.

"You ready?" Beau asked, lacing his fingers through mine.

I turned and walked back down the aisle, nodding and speaking to others who made their way to pay their condolences. Beau stood quietly and patiently beside me. I noticed several people curiously flick their gazes at the town's black sheep stationed beside me. This would be all over town before the night was over. Somehow that didn't matter right then. Beau had been my friend since he'd pulled my hair on the playground and I in return grabbed his hand and twisted his arm behind his back. After the preschool teacher corrected us both and threatened to call our parents, Beau had looked over at me and asked, "Want to sit by me and my cousin at lunch?"

They could all talk. Beau had come to my rescue when I needed rescuing the most. He might not be the perfect citizen, but Grana always said perfect was boring. She would love that I'd snubbed my nose at the gossiping betties at her funeral. I glanced back over my shoulder, smiling. She was there somewhere, and I could almost hear her laughter as I walked out of the church holding Beau's hand.

Chapter 10

ASHTON

Ashton,

You haven't written me back so either this means my e-mail never got through, which is believable with the unreliable Internet access here, or something is wrong. I tried calling several times, but I can't seem to get any signal out here no matter where I am.

I've got good news and bad news. Bad news is Catherine had an allergic reaction to some unknown plant and she broke out in hives and Dad had to rush her to the nearest town. He just got back an hour ago and she's going to be fine, but Mom is ready to go home.

That leads me to the good news. I'm coming home. We are packing as I write this, and as soon as I'm in cell phone reception range, I'm going to call you. Keep your phone on you. I need to hear your voice. Also, call Beau for me and tell him I'm coming home. He and I can hit the weight room a week early to get ready for football practice. Also, tell him to lay off the beer. I need my best receiver in shape.

Love ya,

Sawyer

I stared at the screen of my laptop for a long time. I wasn't sure what to do. Who to tell. Where to go. Slowly I closed the computer and shoved it off my lap and onto the bed. I'd woken up knowing I was going to have to deal with my parents' questions this morning about leaving the church with Beau last night. It was something I had dreaded, but this was much worse. The screen on my phone lit up before "Eye of the Tiger" began to play for the first time in three weeks. Sawyer had put "Eye of the Tiger" on my phone to be his special ring. Numbly I reached for it and pressed the accept button before lifting it to my ear.

"Hello?"

"Ahhh, man, baby, is it good to hear your voice. Did you get my e-mail? I waited to call until I thought you might be awake. We're about two hours away. I'm having Dad drop me off at your house. I can't wait to see you." Guilt, frustration, anger, and panic all seemed to whirl around inside me at once. My grip on the phone tightened as I took several deep breaths.

"Um, hey, yeah, I just got your e-mail. I can't believe y'all are coming home early." The lack of enthusiasm in my voice was unmistakable. A second of silence ticked by, and I knew Sawyer's brain was working overtime.

"Did you just wake up? You don't sound real happy about my coming home. I expected squeals of delight or something."

Perfect, make him suspicious before he even gets here. I needed to fix this. I couldn't come between Beau and Sawyer. They'd been as close as brothers all their lives. I'd never be able to forgive myself if I caused a rift between them. The fact that I was worried about Beau and Sawyer's relationship instead of my and Sawyer's surprised me.

"Sorry, I'm thrilled. I just woke up. Last night was Grana's viewing and her funeral is this afternoon. It's been a rough few days."

"What? Ash, baby. Your Grana passed away? Oh, baby, I'm so sorry. Why didn't you tell me?" I'd forgotten he didn't know. The e-mail I never wrote him flashed in my memory. Instead of telling him about Grana, I'd run to Beau. Would any of that have happened if I'd just e-mailed Sawyer and gone with Mom to deal with funeral arrangements that day? Did I wish things had happened differently?

"It wasn't something I wanted to write in an e-mail," I explained, hoping he understood or, at the very least, accepted my excuse.

"I'm coming home. I'll rush to the house and change before I come over so I won't have to leave before the funeral. I can drive you there. It's going to be okay. I'll be there soon. I promise."

How would he feel if I told him things were okay? Beau had helped me say my good-bye already. Beau had held me while I cried. My tears were dried up now. I knew Grana was happy with those fancy streets of gold and a fabulous mansion. She always said God would give her a big ole rose garden she could tend to up there.

"Ash, you okay?"

"I'm sorry. I was thinking about the funeral. I'll see you when you get here."

"Okay. I love you." Those were the words we always said when we hung up the phone. Normally, I was the one who said them first. This time I'd completely forgotten.

"Love you, too," I replied dutifully before hanging up.

I did love him. I always had, just not the way I should. Deep down I'd always known something was wrong between us. Until these last few weeks with Beau, I hadn't really been able to put my finger on what was missing in our relationship. With Beau, I could be me and he loved me. Sawyer loved the me I worked very hard to be. If Sawyer knew the real me, the girl he thought I'd left behind with my childhood, he'd never love me. He couldn't. But I couldn't be with Beau. I could never choose him over Sawyer. It would rip apart a lifetime of friendship. Sawyer had been the one to take care of Beau as a kid. He looked out for him and shared his wealth with him. Even now Sawyer guarded Beau from so many things. Just last year the coach was going to kick Beau off the football team for showing up to practice with a hangover. Sawyer had begged the coach and promised to personally make sure Beau walked the straight and narrow on practice and game days. Beau needed Sawyer. I couldn't get between them.

I threw the pillow I'd been squeezing in my arms across the room and growled in frustration. This was ridiculous. I was ridiculous. *How could I have let myself do this? What had I been thinking?* I'd let myself care too much about Beau Vincent. I didn't just care about him; I wanted him. It was the worst thing in the world I could've done. Having him meant ripping away the only family he cared about. I'd have the whole town talking about him and hating him for stealing Sawyer's girl. It was impossible. The whole stupid situation.

"Honey, are you awake?" Dad's voice called from the other

side of my closed door. I let out a sigh. This was the talk I'd been dreading: the pointless talk, the one he didn't even have to waste his breath on.

"Yeah, Dad, come in," I replied.

My door opened, and there he stood with the small frown on his face I rarely saw directed at me. He walked inside and stopped at the end of my bed. His arms were crossed over his chest, and I could smell his aftershave. The same kind he'd been wearing all my life.

"What exactly happened last night?" He was direct and to the point. I had to give him that. I sat up straight on my bed and stared right back at him. I needed to cover this up. Smooth it over. Beau's acceptance in this town and his relationship with Sawyer depended on it.

"I take it you're referring to Beau Vincent?" As if I had to ask this. Dad's eyebrows shot up as if he thought I might be losing my mind to even think he could be referring to something else.

"Yes, Ashton, I am."

I sighed, shook my head, and even threw in an eye roll for dramatic effect. "Beau's my friend. We grew up together. He's my boyfriend's cousin and best friend. Sawyer wasn't there, I was dealing with one of the hardest things in my life, and Beau showed up to step in and help me. He loves Sawyer and knew it was what Sawyer would've wanted him to do. Besides,

Beau knows how close I was to Grana. He used to sit on her porch and eat her cookies with me. Remember, back then when the fact that his mama was a cocktail waitress at a bar wasn't an issue?"

The bitterness in my voice was unavoidable. Dad's eyebrows snapped together. He didn't like my tone of voice, but I could see he was thinking about my excuse. I waited, quietly praying he believed it. After what felt like an eternity, he nodded and let out a heavy sigh.

"I understand this has been hard on you. With Sawyer gone and your mom and me busy dealing with funeral arrangements and relatives coming in from out of town, we haven't been here for you. I appreciate the fact Beau noticed you needed someone and stepped in. However, Beau Vincent isn't the kind of boy I want you associating with. He's Sawyer's cousin and when Sawyer's around, then it's fine. But Beau isn't from good stock. His daddy was a wild card and his mama's white trash. You can get a bad reputation spending time with the likes of him. Bad company corrupts good character. Remember that."

I wanted to stand up and yell to the rooftops that he didn't know anything about Beau's stock. It didn't matter who his parents were. Blaming the child for the parents' sins was wrong. Didn't the Bible he read daily discuss judging people and forgiveness? I bit down on my tongue until I tasted blood in an attempt to keep from screaming out in frustration.

"Who called you so early?" Dad asked, eyeing the phone I'd thrown down beside my pillow.

"Sawyer," I said. Obvious relief washed over his face. He really needed to get out of here before I lost it.

"Really? How's he doing?"

"He's on his way home. He'll be here in time for the funeral."

Dad smiled brightly, making a sick knot form in my stomach.

"Well, good, good. I'm glad he's coming home for Grana's funeral. He's such a good boy." With a pleased look, Dad turned and left the room, closing my door behind him. I glared at the shut door the way I wish I could have glared at him.

I pulled the car onto the gravel driveway before cutting the ignition. Beau's truck was the only vehicle parked outside his trailer. His mother wasn't there. That was the only good thing about this visit. I needed to do this alone. Sawyer would be in town within the next thirty minutes. I'd have come sooner, but after my talk with Dad this morning, I decided it was best to wait until he left for the church.

My chest hurt. I pressed the palm of my hand against my heart, trying to ease the pain. There had to be a limit to the amount of heartbreak one person could suffer in a week. Surely, God could see I'd met my limit? I needed a miracle. A bitter laugh bubbled up inside me at the thought of God helping me with this situation. God didn't help girls get the bad boys. But

Beau wasn't bad inside. Not really. He acted the only way he knew how. He was raised by a waitress at a bar who jumped from one man's bed to another regardless of his marital status. No one had tried to teach Beau the right way to act. Inside he was a wonderful person. He was caring, sensitive, funny, patient, and understanding. He was accepting. Something no one in my life had ever been other than Grana.

The door on the trailer swung open, and Beau stepped out onto the top step and stared out at me. The only thing on his body was a pair of low riding jeans. Even his feet were bare. I swallowed the tears in my throat. I had gone there to end things, and it felt like my heart was being ripped out of my body before I'd even said a word. As if in slow motion, I reached for the door handle of my car and stepped out onto the gravel. Our eyes met as I closed the door.

A frown replaced the sexy smile on his face. He could read me so well. He'd always known what I was thinking. When we were kids, I never had to tell him when I was upset. He knew it and he was trying to fix it before Sawyer had a clue my fragile female feelings had been injured. He didn't move. Instead he watched me as I put one foot in front of the other, wishing more than anything in the world I didn't have to do this. Just this once I wanted to be selfish and take what I wanted. Forget about the repercussions and throw myself into Beau's arms. I wanted to tell him I loved him. I wanted to kiss his face right there, standing in front of his trailer, for anyone who had their noses pressed to their windows to see. I wanted to claim Beau as mine, but I couldn't do any of those things. Our fairy tale would never work. He'd lose Sawyer. The town would hate him instead of just mumbling about him turning out just like his dad. My father would never accept him. I'd probably be locked in my room or sent off to an all-girls' school. No one would allow this. I couldn't let Beau know why. He was braver than I was. He would fight for me. He would lose what little he had in this stupid town for me, and for nothing. My parents would never let it happen. I had to let him go. What I wanted wasn't important. Beau's future was.

"Something tells me this isn't the kind of visit I'd been hoping for when I saw that little white car pull up." His voice sounded tight.

I fought to keep the tears stinging the back of my eyes from rolling down my face. I had to do this. It was for the best. Beau's best.

"He's coming home today," I said through the thickness in my throat.

Beau stepped back and motioned for me to step inside. I dropped my gaze from his and walked into his trailer for the second and last time. I'd never be able to come back. Not with Sawyer. I wouldn't be able to forget the breakfast we'd shared over his kitchen table. The laughter and the way his jaw worked when he chewed. I'd been fascinated watching him eat that morning.

The door closed behind me, and I stood staring at the empty table. A box of opened cereal sat on the table by an empty bowl. Beau's arms slipped around my waist. I knew I should step away, but I couldn't make myself. This was home. Being in his arms like this was where I found peace. Knowing this was the last time he would ever touch me made the moment bittersweet. I inhaled deeply soaking in his smell, his warmth, the feel of his hands against my stomach.

"We knew this day was coming. It's just sooner than expected. I've been thinking about it, and I want you to let me talk to him. I think I can."

"No," I said, stopping him. I had to say something before he said too much. His planning was pointless. There was nothing to plan.

He turned me around to face him then slipped his hands through my hair. I watched helplessly as his head lowered until his lips touched mine. I knew I needed to stop him, but all I could do was kiss him back greedily. The soft rumbling moan in his chest made my knees weak. Closing my eyes tightly, I pushed away from him.

"I can't be with you, Beau." I didn't open my eyes. Seeing his face as I said the words I knew had to be said would kill me. He didn't speak or reach out to touch me. I knew he was waiting on me to finish. I took a shaky breath. "I love Sawyer. I can't hurt him. I'm sorry." There was so much more I wanted to say. So many things I'd practiced on the way over here, but the lump in my throat was fighting against me.

"Okay," he replied in almost a whisper.

Slowly I lifted my head and opened my eyes to see his face. "Okay" wasn't exactly what I'd expected from him. My breath caught as I took in his expression. He didn't look hurt. He didn't even appear upset. Instead he looked . . . bored. I was fighting off the need to snot cry all over myself and he was completely unfazed. There was no relief. My heart shattered.

Could it all have meant so little to him? He'd said he loved me. Why would he lie about that? I watched as he pulled his phone out of his pocket and started texting someone. I wanted to scream at him to show some emotion. To show me he cared for me. That this was hard for him, too. I'd thought he would fight for me.

His hazel eyes lifted to glance at me. "I need to make a call. If that's all you needed . . ." He nodded his head toward the door as if asking me to leave. Numbly I walked past him without a word. He didn't even say good-bye.

Chapter 11

BEAU

The moment I heard Ashton's car crank, I threw my phone against the wall. It fell to the floor in pieces. I knew how it felt. Shattered. Broken. Destroyed. I'd been so sure she loved me. Even though she'd never uttered the words, I'd been so damn sure she wanted me—not my perfect, polished cousin. Never before in my life had I hated Sawyer, but right now, I hated him. I hated him for taking her. I hated him for controlling her. I hated him because he had her love.

A roar filled the room, and I barely recognized the angry snarl coming from my mouth. I wouldn't be able to stay here. How could I watch them? How could I go to school and see him touch her? Hold her hand? Oh God, kiss her mouth! Did she care that she'd just destroyed me? Had this all been a little game to her? Pass the time with the bad boy while the prince is away?

"Dammit, Ash."

My mangled cell phone began ringing. Panicked, I thought it could be her, that she could've changed her mind, so I ran over to it and fumbled with the battery, holding it in place while I pressed the accept button several times before it worked. The screen was black.

"Hello?"

"Guess who's home early and ready to get your lazy ass in the gym and pump weights first thing in the morning?" Sawyer's chipper voice came over the line, and I fought the instinct to throw the phone against the wall again. What did I say to him? How did I begin to act like I was happy he was home?

"Beau? You there?"

"Yeah, I'm here."

"What is it with everyone? Could someone act happy about me coming home early?"

I tamped down the small ray of hope trying to break into my thoughts. Surely, he didn't mean Ashton.

"I'm sure your . . . Ash is happy you're back," I said. I wondered if he'd noticed I'd stopped myself from calling her his girlfriend. I wasn't ready to accept that. He let out a frustrated sigh.

"No, she seemed distracted. I just found out about Grana. Man, I hate that I wasn't here. I guess she's upset about that, and

I'm being selfish, wishing she'd acted happy about seeing me. Have you seen her? Is she doing okay?"

I had to be careful. She'd made her decision. That didn't mean I couldn't change her mind, but I had to protect her.

"She's upset. We've bumped into each other some. She helped me and Nicole out one night when I'd had too much to drink. Gave us a ride home. I also went to the church last night to pay my respects and all. I remember Grana. She was good to me."

Sawyer sighed. "Thanks, man. I appreciate you going. I know it meant a lot to Ash."

I slammed my fist against the wall. I didn't need him to thank me. I hadn't done it for him.

"Well, I'll see ya at the funeral then?"

No, I wasn't ready to see them together. Watching Sawyer touch her might send me into a blind rage at Grana's funeral.

"I got some stuff to do. I went last night, but you're back and I did my duty."

"Okay. Well, thanks again. I'm not kidding about the weight room tomorrow morning. I need to get your beer gut in shape."

"Sure, see ya then."

I dropped the broken pieces of my phone onto the coffee table. I needed to make a plan. I needed to think about this. Had I screwed up by letting her go? Had she wanted me to stop her? Ashton Gray was going to drive me mad.

ASHTON

"You told Sawyer he was welcome to come eat with us tonight, didn't you?"

Dad stood at the door of my bedroom. I'd come home from the funeral and gone straight into the shower so I could cry in private. Once the water ran cold, I'd dried my tears and forced myself to get a grip. *What would Grana have told me to do? Would she have told me to go with my heart? Or would she have seen the wisdom in my decision?* I thought back to the way Beau had reacted to my words. What had I expected him to do? Fall at my feet in tears? I should be happy he'd handled it so well. I didn't need hurting him to add to my guilt.

"Yes. He'll be here at six." I sat up from my reclined position on my bed. Dad seemed pleased with that answer.

"You've been so closed off from the world this summer. I'm really relieved Sawyer's home."

I forced a smile so Dad wouldn't guess anything was amiss. He walked away and closed my door behind him. I lay back on the bed and stared at the ceiling, wondering how I was going to face Sawyer with the guilt of what I'd done weighing on me so heavily.

I loved Sawyer. My actions didn't appear as if I did, but I did love him. The problem was that I wasn't in love with him. I hadn't realized there were different kinds of love you could feel for a boy. Sawyer was everything I respected. He was sweet and caring. I never had to worry he would leave me or hurt me. He was impossible not to love. Unfortunately, he had a girlfriend who was a big huge fake. He deserved to know what a fake I was, but how did I go about explaining to him that I put on a show for him, for my parents, for the whole dang town? I couldn't tell Sawyer anything. Word in a small town got around fast. My mother would be devastated. My dad would be furious. I'd hurt them both, and for what? A guy who didn't even care enough to respond to me when I broke things off with him? My heart had been breaking and he had been texting someone. Probably Nicole. The thought of Beau with Nicole made me nauseous.

"Here, let me clean this up. You haven't seen Sawyer in weeks. Go on ahead and go. I know you want to spend some time together." This wasn't my dad. He normally wanted us to stay right here under their watch or at least out on the front porch. Rarely did he encourage us to go off and spend time together. Apparently, he was more worried about Beau than I'd thought. But then, he had reasons to be worried about Beau. Maybe it was a parent's intuition.

Sawyer stood up with his plate and cup in his hands, always the gentleman. Not only did he clean up his spot at the table, but he rinsed his used dishes in the sink. Samantha Vincent had trained her son well. Or at least that was what Mom always said.

"Thank you, both, for dinner. It was delicious." Sawyer smiled at my parents, then turned to me and winked before taking his dishes to the dishwasher. He wasn't as tall as Beau. I'd never really paid attention to that before. They had so many similarities in their appearance, but they were so different. Sawyer's dark brown hair was long enough that it brushed his collar and curled along the ends. His lips weren't as full as Beau's, but his shoulders were broader. They'd always joked that he had the stronger arm when it came to throwing a football, but Beau had the stronger arm when it came to throwing a punch. I glanced down at Mom, who was smiling the silly happy smile she has when Sawyer's around. The guilt in my chest grew. She would never smile over me being with Beau.

"Such a good boy," she said.

I forced my hundredth smile of the night and nodded.

Sawyer walked up beside me and took my hand.

"I'll have her home by eleven, sir," he said, looking at my dad.

"Oh, don't worry about the time. I know you two have a lot of catching up to do."

Sawyer appeared as surprised as I was. If I didn't know better, I'd think Dad was popping some of Mom's anxiety pills.

The moment Sawyer closed the door to his shiny, one-year-old Dodge truck, he reached over and took my hand to pull me up beside him. There was no stick shift in the way in Sawyer's truck.

"God, I've missed you," he whispered before grabbing my

face and kissing me softly on the mouth. It was just as nice as I'd remembered. Sweet and gentle and very comfortable. I reached up and threaded my fingers through his thick hair and tried out some of my new kissing moves on him to see if I could get the earth-shattering sensation Beau's kisses always produced. Sawyer made a sound that reminded me of a growl and dropped his hands to my waist to pull me closer to him. But still, it just remained . . . nice.

Finally he pulled back, breathing hard, and rested his forehead on mine.

"That was . . . wow." I smiled, wishing I could agree. "If I'd been forced to stay away from you another week, I think I'd have lost it. I love my family, but I was having serious Ashton withdrawal." The guilt inside me twisted cruelly. Tears stung my eyes, and I laid my head on his chest. He was just so good.

"Ash, something is wrong. I could see it inside when we were at the table. You looked so sad, and your parents are acting differently."

"Losing Grana was a shock. A hard blow to all of us. I think Dad might have slipped one or two of Mom's anxiety meds because I'll agree he's acting odd. But I'm just dealing. I'm sorry. I'm so depressing and you just got home."

He squeezed my shoulder. "It's okay. I understand."

He backed out of the driveway and headed toward his house. We were going down to the hole. I didn't have to ask. It was secluded and safe. He'd probably call his dad and let him know we were back there, just to make sure all his bases were covered. Parking wasn't something we would ever be caught doing. It would sully his reputation and we couldn't have that. I could hear the mocking tone in my thoughts and I closed my eyes to silently scold myself. The bad girl might not go back in her cage without a fight this time.

The truck jostled us around as we made our way slowly over the unpaved path. There was no light out at the hole. The lights from the truck lit up the dirt road, and different small animals scurried out of our way. Once we broke through the tree-covered path, the moonlight shimmered on the water ahead. Sawyer came to a stop. His hand reached up and shut off the engine before he tilted his head down to gaze at me.

"I'm sorry I wasn't here, Ash. Losing Grana like that had to be awful. Are you mad at me for being away?" Not what I needed—Sawyer feeling guilty when he had absolutely no reason to. It made me feel like pond scum.

"Of course I'm not mad at you, Sawyer. I wish you could have returned to a happy, cheerful girlfriend. You don't deserve this."

He patted my knee and I studied his hand. It wasn't as big as Beau's or as tanned.

"It's okay. I know the old Ash will show up again once you

finish mourning." He paused and I glanced up at him. A small frown line appeared on his forehead. Something was bothering him. I'd known him most of my life and I knew that look.

"A few of the ladies from church mentioned Beau holding your hand at the wake." He let out a forced chuckle. "It bothered them and they thought I should know."

I didn't panic. I got angry. Stupid busybodies. This was exactly what I'd known would happen. Everyone would jump on the Sawyer bandwagon and start bad-mouthing Beau. Like Beau needed them to dislike him any more than they already did. I wanted to howl in frustration, but I took a calming breath and counted backward from ten in my head. Every once in a while the counting thing took the edge off. When I was sure I could respond without sounding livid, I said the first thing that came to my mind.

"When we were kids, Beau was just as close to me as you were. He sat on Grana's porch just as many times as you did. He ate Grana's cookies and played Uno with her just like you did. She was a part of his childhood. One of the few bright spots. He knew you were gone, and he knew I would be devastated. So he came to the church and asked me if I'd gone up to see her. I admitted I hadn't and wasn't sure I could. He then encouraged me to go say my good-byes and said he'd walk with me. I guess he saw the fear in my eyes, so he reached down and took my hand. Then we walked together to the front of the church.

He let my hand go and stepped back while I had my last few moments of closure with Grana. Then he took my hand and walked me out of the church because, like you, he knows when I'm about to lose it. And he knows the little girl inside enough to know I didn't want to break down in front of everyone and have them hovering around me."

We sat in silence for a few minutes. I'd heard the anger in my tone. No doubt he had too.

"Remind me to thank him for watching out for my girl. I owe him one. It's about time you two realized you were best friends for most of your life. I always felt a little guilty that it had ended."

There he went again, talking about how he felt guilty. I just wanted to go home and bury myself under the covers. This was too much to deal with right then. The guilt, the anger, the frustration, and the pain: They were all going to drive me insane.

Chapter 12

ASHTON

We walked toward the bonfire. I'd decided against telling Sawyer about Ryan's stupid, drunken episode last week. It was over now, and it hadn't been so bad after all. Of course, Ryan touching me was gross, but I'd ended the evening with Beau playing pool. The memory of him grinning at me across the pool table as I set up my shot caused my heart to ache. I missed him so much.

As we made our way into the clearing, several people stopped Sawyer and welcomed him home. Everyone wanted to talk football. I smiled and appeared to be waiting patiently while scanning the crowd for Beau. I hadn't seen him since I'd walked out of his trailer without a good-bye. Every night since then I'd lain in my bed, holding my phone and willing him to call or at least text me. But he hadn't. The idea that things would go back to the way they had been before terrified me. I couldn't be with him the way I wanted to, but I didn't want to lose everything. My anger at the way he'd dismissed me had dimmed. I just wanted to see him. Talk to him. See him smile at me.

"Come on, I see Beau and Nicole over there," Sawyer said as he slipped his hand behind my back and led me over to a small group of football players and their girlfriends. The group was sitting on the tailgate of a few trucks and three old tractor tires they'd hauled out here years ago. A small fire crackled in the middle of the group, putting a warm glow on all their faces.

"Sawyer. The man has returned," said Ethan Payne, grinning from his spot on the tailgate of his truck. Brooke Milery snuggled up against him and lifted a hand to wiggle her bright pink nails at us in greeting. They'd broken up last spring, but, apparently, they were back together or heading in that direction. Her legs were draped over his lap and his hand was tucked snugly between her thighs.

"Come, talk to us. Tell us how you're going to lead us to state," said Toby Horn.

"I'm not the one who nailed the win at the last state game," Sawyer reminded him as he leaned against the truck and pulled me back against him.

Toby played cornerback. He'd intercepted a pass at the state championship game last year and made the game-winning touchdown after jumping over two tackles. After the game, his status level had risen, which would explain why the head cheerleader, Kayla Jenkins, was sitting on his lap. She'd been determined to get Beau's attention last year. It appeared as if she had moved on.

"You know, that's right. I think we need to make sure coach gives our star corner some more wide-receiver action," Ethan piped in.

"Agreed," Sawyer replied.

They continued to talk football, but I couldn't pay attention. Beau was directly across from me. It was taking all my willpower not to look at him. I smiled and tried not to appear stiff, although I felt uncomfortable with Sawyer's arms wrapped around my waist. Sawyer leaned down and kissed my temple casually while he talked. I heard something about a blitz and upping the practice time. But all my focus was on not staring at Beau.

"Earth to Ashton." Kayla's voice broke into my thoughts. I jerked my head up and stared directly at her. She seemed to be waiting on me to reply.

"Um, I didn't hear you, sorry," I said, feeling the blush creep up my neck.

She giggled and twirled a long red curl around her finger.

"I asked you if you wanted to be one of the spirit girls.

Maybe this year our quarterback will actually accept a spirit girl if he gets to choose you."

Spirit girls were girls the cheerleaders added to their numbers so every football player would have a girl to make him goodies on game day. Off the record, spirit girls also happened to help their players with their homework, order pizzas to be delivered to the school for their lunches, and do some unofficial things like back massages and other "hands-on" activities. The starters always picked their spirit girl first, then the rest of the players' names went into a hat and the spirit girls drew them.

"Um, yes, of course," I replied.

Sawyer chuckled. "Then Ash is mine."

Kayla smiled, but she seemed more annoyed than amused. "We're assigning each girl two players this year. So you'll have one more boy to take care of. The boys haven't picked yet, but I doubt anyone else chooses you since you're Sawyer's. You'll have to draw a name."

Nicole laughed, and I instantly tensed, preparing for her rude comment.

Without thinking, I glanced over toward the sound of her laughter and immediately wished I hadn't. Beau was sitting on the ground and leaning up against a tractor tire, his legs bent and wide open. Right in between his muscular jean-clad legs sat Nicole. She had one arm wrapped around his neck and the other one resting on his knee. It would have been easier if she'd just stood up and punched me in the gut or maybe whacked me around a few times. At the moment the pain would be a welcome distraction to the tightness taking over my chest.

Beau's eyes locked on mine. After everything we'd been through together, I hoped I would see some small shred of . . . oh . . . I don't know. Just something. But he didn't look fazed by me at all. It was as if those two weeks had never happened. I swallowed the lump in my throat.

"You know, Ashton, I've always wondered what it is you do so right to keep Sawyer on such a tight leash. I mean, you've got to be hiding some hidden talent from us." Nicole's words were slurred, but they were loud, and I was positive everyone—even people not in the little group surrounding us—had heard her. My stomach turned and twisted. God, I hoped I didn't get sick.

"It isn't one thing, Nic. She's perfect at everything she does." Sawyer's voice sounded as calm and nice as always.

Nicole snarled. "Doubt that. You've just forgotten what a good time feels like."

Sawyer tensed, and his arms tightened around me as if he were protecting me. I'd always wondered what Sawyer had done with Nicole in the seventh grade. At times I'd been jealous when she looked at him, as if she knew him in ways that I didn't. But then, he was so careful not to do anything other than kiss me. I figured he had to be as chaste as I was—"was" being the important word.

"Shut up, Nicole." The words hadn't been Sawyer's. Beau's deeper voice had snapped out the order. Nicole giggled again and leaned forward to shake her braless boobs at Sawyer.

"You remember how much fun it was, don't ya, Saw? We had lots of fun," she slurred.

"Shut the hell up, Nicole." Beau growled angrily, pushing her away from him. I should be hurt that my boyfriend wasn't as inexperienced as I'd thought. The fact he'd been unable to keep his hands off Nicole and didn't have any problem not touching me should bother me. It didn't. All I felt was relief at seeing Beau pushing Nicole off him.

"What's the matter? You don't like hearing about how your cousin had me first? Hmm . . . don't be jealous, baby. You're the only one who's getting in my pants tonight." Nicole attempted to purr, but her slurring kind of made it sound more like she was moaning.

Sawyer moved from behind me and took my arm to pull me away. I felt Beau's eyes on me, and I glanced back at him. In that moment I could see the Beau I'd thought loved me. As he pushed Nicole away absently, his eyes said he was sorry. Not once did he break eye contact with me as Sawyer led me into the pecan orchard. There was that pain in those eyes that had haunted my dreams. I gave him a sad smile before turning to follow my boyfriend into the shadows of the trees. The light from the fire disappeared as did the noise. The moon managed to peek through the branches, shedding enough light to keep us from walking into a tree or tripping over a fallen branch.

"Ash, I'm so sorry," Sawyer said, pulling me into his arms once we got to his truck. "She's a vile human being, and why I ever dated her I don't know. I wish Beau would get rid of her." He kissed the top of my head like I was a child he needed to comfort. I didn't feel like crying. But I wanted to know why. For so long I had thought he was without sin and I was the one who needed to be tamed, but that hadn't been true.

"Did you have sex with her, Sawyer?" I asked, staring up at him. The guilty expression on his face answered my question for me. He cupped the side of my face with his hand.

"Ash, it was a long time ago. She was my first girlfriend, and although she was pretty wild for a thirteen-year-old, we were still young. Of course we didn't have sex," he said.

"You obviously did something. You hardly touch me, yet it sounds like you did a lot more than kissing with Nicole."

Sawyer frowned. He hadn't been expecting me to voice my feelings. I normally assured him when he was upset. I never wanted to ruffle his feathers. Making life easy for Sawyer had been my mantra for so long. Well, that part of the charade I was living was long gone. No more patting him on the back.

"Ashton, I made some bad decisions with Nicole. She pushed me to do some things. I gave in. But you, you're different. You're good. It isn't about sex with us."

How could you be in love with someone and not want sex? We were human. He was a teenage boy, for crying out loud. He had hormones.

"Are you not attracted to me that way? I mean, I know I don't have Nicole's body and I won't be winning any beauty contests, but if you love me, then I would think sex with me would appeal to you."

Three weeks ago I wouldn't have had the nerve to say these things. Being with Beau had changed me so much.

Sawyer's expression was somewhere between shock and confusion.

"Ashton, I respect you. You deserve respect. You're everything I've ever wanted. You're not just some girl I'm filling my high school years with. I intend to marry you one day."

Marry him? What? Really? Oh god.

He smiled at the shocked expression on my face. "I love you, Ashton. I intend to keep you forever. I'm very attracted to you. I just don't want my future wife to lose her virginity in the bed of a truck."

Chapter 13

ASHTON

The parking lot at the school was almost empty. Only a few parked cars remained. I recognized Sawyer's truck, as well as Beau's. They would both still be at practice. I'd put off going home for over an hour. Sawyer was in the weight room and he hadn't responded to my last text. Going home wasn't something I could handle just yet. My aunt Caroline and her daughter, Lana, had descended upon our house last night and were staying for an undetermined amount of time. Uncle Nolan had been caught doing things he shouldn't with his secretary on top of the copy machine, and Aunt Caroline had fled their home in Georgia. We were the "only place she could think of," and didn't that make us lotto winners? Aunt Caroline cried and regaled anyone who would listen about what she'd found my uncle doing. Hearing it the first time was hard enough; I really didn't want to keep suffering through the recaps. And having Lana invade my personal space was beyond frustrating. She was so polite and polished. I wanted to scream or possibly mess up her hair and slap her around until she showed some emotion.

Leann had left for college already, Sawyer was always busy with football, and Beau was acting like I didn't exist. It was times like that when I felt so alone and lost I'd run to my Grana's so she could make everything right again. Life was unfair.

"What did your car do wrong?"

Beau's voice startled me. I spun around to find him only a few feet behind me, with his helmet and shoulder pads in one hand and the shirt he should be wearing in the other. Lordy, did he have to walk around shirtless? He shifted his gaze from my car to my face. I shuffled my feet nervously. We hadn't been alone in sixteen—no, make that seventeen—days.

"You've been standing here glowering at your car for five minutes. I'm assuming it somehow offended you."

Tears stung my eyes. Being this close to him and having him actually look at me and speak directly to me was wonderful and so incredibly painful.

"What's wrong, Ash?"

Swallowing the lump in my throat didn't help. I bit down on my bottom lip and shrugged. He stood there silently for a moment. I could see the indecision on his face. Finally he reached for my book bag and touched my waist.

"Come with me. You can talk and I'll listen."

I didn't argue. I wanted this. I needed him. I let him guide me to his truck and he opened the passenger door so I could climb in.

We didn't speak at first. I worked on getting my emotions under control while he turned his truck down a familiar road I knew led to our spot on the bay.

"You wanna tell me what's got you upset?" he asked.

He glanced at me for a second but quickly shifted his eyes back to the road. I wasn't sure how to answer that question. A lot of things were wrong. I was with Sawyer, acting like someone I wasn't, someone I'd realized I didn't even like. School had started back, and Beau was there every day in the halls, in the cafeteria, and in my classrooms. I could see him and not touch him. It was killing me. Then, of course, my aunt Caroline and Lana were taking away the only refuge I had left: my house, my room.

"Come on, Ash, tell me what's going on."

"My uncle cheated on my aunt, and now my aunt and my cousin have moved into my house. Lana is in my room all the time. I have no privacy. My aunt is crying and retelling the awful story of how she caught him. There's nowhere to hide. I just want to run off into the woods and scream."

The soft chuckle from beside me, him laughing at my predicament, should have ticked me off, but I'd missed the sound so much it made me smile.

"Family can be a bitch," he said a little somberly. I wondered if he was talking about Sawyer. Did he care I was with Sawyer? I couldn't tell. I wanted to believe he was hiding his feelings from me, but it seemed very unlikely. He laughed and flirted with every pretty face at school just like he'd always done.

"So I found you standing a few feet away from your car, glaring at it like it had teeth and was going to bite you, because you didn't want to go home?"

I thought about admitting I missed him, that I'd fought the urge daily to get in my car and ride down to the bar where he'd taken me to play pool, hoping to find him.

He patted the spot beside him, and I scooted over without hesitation. His hand found mine, and he squeezed it. For the first time since Sawyer had come home, I felt complete. Being with Beau made me believe everything would be okay, that the issues keeping us apart wouldn't always matter, and everything would eventually turn out all right.

We pulled onto our piece of land overlooking the Mobile Bay. Everything seemed so different in the sunlight. He released my hand, and I started to scoot away, when his arm slid behind me to pull me closer to his side. I let out a contented sigh and rested my head in the crook of his arm.

Neither of us spoke. We just sat there in silence and watched the sun set over the water.

My eyes began to droop and I smiled, thinking how easy everything was with him.

"Ash." Beau's breath tickled my ear. My eyes flew open, and it took me a moment to remember where I was. Rubbing the sleep out of my eyes, I slowly sat up.

"I fell asleep," I mumbled.

Beau chuckled. "Yeah you did."

"I'm sorry. I didn't mean to."

Beau tucked a strand of hair behind my ear and flashed me the crooked smile that never failed to make my heart flutter.

"Don't be. I can't think of a better time I've had since . . . well, since . . ."

What did he mean by that? Since when? Since this summer when it'd been just us? Before he'd let me walk out of his trailer without an argument?

"I need to get you back. Sawyer's texted your phone and called you several times. The last time he called, I figured it was time I woke you—even though I enjoyed having you sleep on me."

My heart thumped against my chest. Hearing him say things like that to me gave me hope. Hope for what, I didn't know. I'd been the one to decide it wasn't worth it. He handed me my phone.

"Answer him. This is going to be hard enough to explain as it is."

I read both texts from him asking me where I was at. He sounded concerned in his last one. The fact that my car was still in the school parking lot was bothering him.

Beau's phone rang, and he glanced down at it and frowned. "It's Sawyer."

I reached for his phone. "Here, let me answer it. I might as well explain. Besides, we did nothing wrong."

"Hello?"

"Ash? Where are you? Why're you answering Beau's phone? I've been trying to call you."

"I'm sorry. I know. I was just about to call you. I've been asleep. Beau found me in the parking lot. I didn't want to go home and face all the drama. He offered to listen to me rant some, and I ended up falling asleep. He let me sleep. But he's bringing me back to my car now."

Sawyer was quiet for a moment. I glanced over at Beau, who was watching me with an expression that reminded me of a lion that sensed danger and was getting ready to pounce.

"Okay, I'll go wait for you at your car," he finally replied.

I wasn't sure what Sawyer was thinking by the tone of his voice. Normally, I could gauge his mood over the phone.

"I'll see you in a little while then," I said, and handed the phone back to Beau.

He closed it and nodded toward the passenger side of the truck.

"If he's going to be waiting on us, you probably need to scoot over. I'm not sure he'd be that understanding."

Beau cranked the truck and turned it back toward town. Reluctantly, I slid back over to the far side of the truck. Away from his warmth.

"Beau . . . thank you. I needed this. I needed, I needed . . . you."

He let out a heavy sigh and shook his head. "Saying things like that to me makes this so damn hard. I'll always be here for you. But don't tell me you need me."

"But I can't help it. I do."

"Dammit, Ash. I can't listen to that. I can't think about it. I can deal with denying myself what I need. What I want. But I can't deny you."

"You love Sawyer. He's like your brother. Could you really hurt him that way? Could you really lose him over a girl? I don't know if I could let you do it. One day you would resent me for coming between the two of you. You would never be able to love me. I would always be a reminder of how I was the reason you lost Sawyer." I laid my head back on the seat and closed my eyes. There were so many reasons why I could never have Beau. And every time I voiced one, it ripped another hole in my heart.

"You're right," he said in a hoarse whisper.

Hearing him agree felt as if he'd just ran a sword through my chest. I bit back a sob and turned my head away from him.

Neither of us spoke again.

When he pulled into the parking spot beside my car, Sawyer was at the passenger side of Beau's truck, immediately opening it and reaching for me.

"I'm sorry, baby. I've been so wrapped up in football that I've been ignoring you. You just lost Grana and now your relatives have invaded your house." He pulled me into his arms and I let him hug me. Right now my chest ached so badly that I needed someone to hold me together. Even if that someone wasn't Beau.

"Thank you, Beau. You were there for her when I wasn't. I owe you one," Sawyer said over my head. I didn't look at Beau. I kept my face buried in Sawyer's chest.

"You're welcome," he replied. Sawyer closed the truck door, and I listened as the tires crunched over the gravel: the sound of Beau driving off and leaving me here with Sawyer.

"Come back to my house with me. I'm grilling outside with Dad tonight and my parents would love to have you over," Sawyer said, pulling back to gaze down at me. I couldn't say no. I didn't want to say no. Going home meant more Lana and more Aunt Caroline.

"Okay."

Chapter 14

BEAU

"Hey, Beau."

I turned around to see Kayla walking up beside me with a clipboard in her hands. The halls were packed with everyone stopping by their locker in between classes. This would be the time Kayla hunted me down to ask me a question. It was impossible to get away from her in this crowd. She gave me a flirty smile and licked her lips. Kayla was brave enough to speak to me only when Nicole was nowhere around.

"Kayla," I replied, and kept walking, forcing her to jog a little to keep up with me. Normally clipboards and Kayla meant that the head cheerleader was going to try to rope you into something.

"You haven't picked your spirit girl yet."

That comment didn't even rank a reply. I never picked my

spirit girl. Someone always ended up doing it. Actually, I normally had several eager and willing volunteers at my locker on game day, begging to meet all my needs.

"I can put your name in the hat for one of the girls to draw your name or you can pick. The rest of the first string has picked already. So several of the girls have their two guys. If you want one of the top picks, you need to claim her now."

Again, no reason to respond.

"Okay, well, here are the best or most popular picks who still have one opening left: Heather Kerr, Blair, Heidi, Noel, Heather Long, and Amy."

Ashton stood beside her locker, trying to appear as if she wasn't listening. I could see her watching me from the corner of her eyes. That caught my attention. The ache that had taken up residence in my chest these days squeezed, reminding me why it was there. Would this feeling ever go away? How long would seeing her hurt so bad?

"Oh, and Ashton, of course." Kayla's chipper tone finally said the one word I couldn't drown out.

"What about Ashton?" I asked, tearing my gaze away from her to stare down at Kayla.

"She's still available. No one has picked her, except Sawyer, of course. I don't think anyone will. No one wants her because they know they won't be getting any special treatment from her. All the special treatment she'll be dishing out will be for Sawyer."

"I want her."

"You do? Really?"

"Yes."

"But you know Noel has a thing for you, and I can promise she'll meet all your needs—" Kayla started saying.

"I want Ashton," I repeated and glared down at her again before turning and heading outside to the field house.

Asking for Ashton might be opening myself up to more pain, but the thought of her doing things for Sawyer was enough to drive me crazy. The thought of her having to bake cookies, decorate a locker, and make cards for another guy infuriated me. Besides, I wasn't doing so great in chemistry. I needed some tutoring. The one-on-one kind where boyfriends weren't allowed.

"That was one helluva catch," Sawyer said as we picked up the discarded helmets we'd thrown on the sidelines before we ran suicides. I didn't look at him as I turned and headed toward the fifty-yard-line to grab the gloves I'd taken off earlier.

"I was a little more focused today," I replied, jogging out to grab my gloves. Sawyer followed me. I needed some distance from him. Today he'd pushed me a little too far with his affection toward Ashton. He, of course, didn't know that.

"I'd started to get worried about you. The last few practices you seemed off. But today you found your sweet spot."

A week ago his comment would have made me feel guilty. But after having to endure him kissing and touching Ashton daily, my guilty conscious was being replaced by rage. *Why the hell should he get to have it all?* Our entire lives he'd had it all, but I'd never cared, never wanted or asked him for anything. Now he has the one thing I want more than air, and he doesn't even know her. The girl he loves doesn't exist.

"Guess I just got rusty this summer," I mumbled.

"Well, you're back. Looked great out there." Sawyer grinned.

His phone beeped, and I forced myself to look away as he checked his text. I hated knowing it was probably Ashton. I hated how badly I wanted to know what she said to him. Did she tell him she loved him? Did she send him little texts asking him to meet her places? Did she make those sexy little moans? Stop it. I had to stop thinking about them together as a couple.

"Hey, Beau, you and Ash got kind of close this summer. I mean, she unloaded on you the other day about her stress at home, and she no longer gets that pinched look on her face when I mention your name, which is a good thing. I'm glad the two people who mean the most to me finally remembered they were once friends."

How do I respond to this? I just nodded.

"Would you, uh, mind doing me a favor? I mean, if you and Nic don't have anything going on tonight. . . . It's just I told Ashton I'd take her out to get something to eat and maybe go to a movie. You know, to get her out of the house and away from the crazy family members. But Dad just texted me, and he needs me to go with him to meet with a friend of his who's in town for the evening and has connections at the university athletic department. It's important, and Dad has worked really hard to set this meeting up. But I don't want to let Ash down either. Could you take her out for me if you aren't already doing something with Nic? Because we both know how she feels about her. I don't want to throw Ash into a situation that makes her uncomfortable."

Did he really just ask me to take Ash out tonight? Was he insane? He didn't deserve her. Any guy who would blow her off for something his daddy wanted shouldn't get to have her.

"Sure," I replied, hearing the clipped tone in my voice. Stupid-ass cousin of mine had no clue what he was asking for. I was already headed for hell; I might as well enjoy the ride.

"Great, thanks, man. Her favorite place to eat is the Seafood Shack. Just meet us there at six. I can grab a drink and spend a few minutes with you guys until I have to head out and meet Dad."

She hated the fried shrimp at the Seafood Shack, and their sweet tea always tasted bitter. It was Sawyer's favorite place, and she had no doubt agreed with him that it was the best place to eat in town. He didn't know her at all.

"Since I'm agreeing to help out, let's do this my way. I

hate the Seafood Shack. I'm sure Princess Ashton won't mind slumming it at Hank's. The burgers there are better than anything the Seafood Shack has, and she really needs to taste their sweet tea."

Sawyer frowned a moment, then he nodded. "Okay, Ash's agreeable. I'm sure she'll be fine with Hank's. I've not taken her there but a couple of times, and I think she might agree with you on the burgers. I remember her scarfing one down."

With bacon and cheese on a toasted bun. She even makes these cute little sounds of pleasure as she eats one. One of the many things I couldn't believe he didn't know about her.

The familiar smell of grease and burgers met me at the door as I stepped inside Hank's. The red-checked Formica tables were already filling up. I nodded at Hank as I passed the grill and made my way to the back. There were more secluded booths in there. I didn't want the whole place watching our every move. If I was going to have Ashton to myself, I wanted to enjoy her without a freaking audience.

I went ahead and ordered Ash's tea and the cheese dip she loved. When Sawyer had texted me to tell me they were on their way, I'd been surprised. Although I'd agreed to this, I hadn't really thought Ashton would. The fact she'd gone along with this had put me in a very good mood.

* * *

ASHTON

"There he is," Sawyer said, taking my hand and leading me to the back of Hank's. My heart sped up at the thought of being in the secluded booth alone with Beau again.

"Hey, man, sorry we're late. I had to drop some flowers off at the nursing home," Sawyer explained. He motioned for me to go in first. I scooted toward the wall and he slid in beside me. Beau slid a glass of sweet tea toward me.

"I haven't been here long. I went ahead and got mine and Ash's drinks, but I didn't order for you. I wasn't sure what you wanted," Beau said.

My favorite cheese dip sat in front of him, and he moved it over toward me as well. "Go ahead and help yourself. I've had all I want of this."

My cheeks became warm remembering the last night we'd shared that cheese dip. It'd been on the way home from our day at the beach.

"I'm good, but thanks. I only have a few minutes, then I've got to go meet Dad," Sawyer said.

Beau glanced at me briefly then turned his attention back to Sawyer.

"Good luck with your meeting."

"Thanks. I'm pumped about it. I hate that I have to leave my girl, but this could be important for my future. I appreciate you hanging out with her tonight."

"Well, you owe me one. Actually, you owe me a few. I also took Ash as my spirit girl today. Someone else was going to get her if I didn't, and I figured you wouldn't want that."

He made it sound as if he were doing Sawyer some big favor. I wasn't a child who needed to be babysat. I didn't come tonight because I couldn't bear to be at home. I'd come because I wanted to be with Beau.

"Just let me know when you want to collect the favors," Sawyer said. "And thanks for picking Ash. I know you could've picked someone else who would've made you happier, but I appreciate you having my back." Sawyer made it seem like Beau hanging out with me and picking me as a spirit girl was some huge sacrifice. It took all my willpower to keep from telling them both to go to Hell and storming out of the restaurant.

"I'll be sure to call them in when I need them," Beau said with a grin on his face that I suddenly wanted to slap off.

"All right, I need to head out," Sawyer said, leaning down to kiss me. I turned my face and glared at the wall behind him, causing his lips to land on my cheek.

"And I'll try not to be too difficult for your cousin," I said with unmistakable anger laced in my voice. Sawyer frowned from my tone. I faked a smile I knew he would believe. That seemed to be enough for him. He nodded and headed out. I waited until the door closed behind him before I turned back around to glower at Beau.

"I'm not some kid who needs pacifying. I can take care of myself. As soon as he's had time to leave the parking lot, I'm going to start walking home."

Beau sat there grinning at me as if I'd just told him he'd won a million dollars.

"God, how I've missed that," he said.

"What?"

"Seeing the real you. You almost unleashed it right here in front of him. I could see the confusion on his face when you let that sexy snarl loose in your voice. Damn, it was hot."

I sat there staring at him, completely confused. Had he made me angry on purpose?

"Are you telling me you baited me? You tried to get me to snap in front of him?" I asked, trying hard to control my temper.

"Ah, and here it comes again, but this time Mr. Perfect isn't here so I'm going to get to see it all full force."

Tears stung my eyes. I'd imagined tonight so much differently. Getting to be alone with Beau and having Sawyer know about it and be okay with it had sounded like a dream come true. Instead Beau decided to treat me like some kind of enjoyable sideshow.

"I'm not here for entertainment purposes, Beau. I agreed to this tonight because, foolishly, I wanted to spend the evening with you. I miss you. And I thought . . . I thought you agreed to it because you missed me, too."

A lump formed in my throat and I grabbed my purse. I needed to get out before I made an idiot of myself and started crying. I was an emotional wreck. I couldn't take Beau hurting me. It was just too much.

"Ash, wait." Beau's words caused me to pause, but I didn't glance back. I would cave in, and then I would be opening myself up to getting hurt some more. I hurried for the door.

Chapter 15

ASHTON

My house was seven miles away, and in the dark, walking very far wouldn't be smart. Besides, Beau would just find me and drive alongside me, trying to get me to get in his stupid truck. I turned and ran down the narrow, paved road leading to the high school. The streetlights lit up the tree-lined road enough to keep it from being spooky. It was less than a mile from Hank's and I could go sit on the bleachers at the football field and have Sawyer pick me up there when he was finished.

My phone dinged, and I glanced at the text message.

Beau: Ash, I'm sorry. Please tell me where ur at.

I clicked ignore and kept heading toward the football field.

Right before I reached the gate entrance, headlights illuminated the darkness behind me. I didn't stop walking. If it was Beau, and I was pretty sure it was, I needed to get away from him. I wanted to cry, and I couldn't cry with him around to watch. His truck door slammed, and I heard his feet running on the gravel. I'd never be able to outrun him, but I could try.

"Ash, I'm sorry." His arms came around me before I could break into a run.

"Beau, let me go. I want to be alone. I'll call Sawyer, and he can pick me up later and take me home."

"No," he replied.

"That wasn't a yes or no question. It was a demand. Now leave."

"Ash, you've got to listen to me. I didn't mean anything I said. I was just trying to see the fire behind your eyes. I've missed it, and I selfishly lashed out knowing you'd get angry. I was wrong, and I'm so, so sorry. Please."

He buried his head in the crook of my neck and took a deep breath. If I had any intention of staying mad at him, it flew right out the window when he did something so vulnerable as nuzzling my neck.

"So you don't consider this a babysitting job in which Sawyer 'owes you one'?" I asked in a much softer tone than I'd been using.

"God no, you know that," he replied, still nuzzling my neck. He threaded his fingers through mine.

"And asking for me as your spirit girl wasn't some great service you did for him? Because I can refuse to do it, and you can ask for another girl."

He stilled, then made a trail of kisses up my neck to my ear.

"The thought of you doing things for Sawyer on game day is hard enough. I couldn't imagine you making cookies for some other guy and decorating his locker and kissing his cheek at the pep rally. The only spirit girl I'll ever want is you."

I turned around in his arms and stared up at him.

"I'm not real strong emotionally right now. With everything going on at home and then coming to school and seeing you. . . ." I stopped explaining. Telling him how much I hated seeing Nicole in his arms and hanging on him wasn't fair. He cupped my face in his hands.

"And I'm the biggest asshole in the world for not thinking about that before treating you the way I did. I'm so sorry, Ash. Please forgive me."

I stood up on my tiptoes and kissed him. "You're forgiven," I whispered, then reluctantly took a step back.

"We should go," I said, then turned to go to his truck.

I didn't scoot over to sit beside him as he pulled out of the parking lot. I glanced down at his hand and noticed the tight grip he had on the stick shift. This wasn't how tonight was supposed to go. I was in Beau's truck again. We were alone and it was okay with Sawyer. I sighed and turned my head to stare out the window and watch the trees pass by as Beau drove back to Hank's.

"Wait here. I'll be right back," he said, then jumped out of the truck and went inside.

He returned seconds later with a takeout bag in his hand.

I watched as he climbed back in the truck and gave me his crooked grin.

"Bacon cheeseburger on a toasted bun," he explained as he held it out to me.

"Thank you," I replied, feeling my heart swell up from the simple fact that he remembered what I liked to eat there.

"I couldn't let you go home tonight without feeding you. Especially after I'd made sure we would be eating somewhere you actually liked. I didn't save you from the Shrimp Shack for nothing."

So that was why Sawyer had changed the location. I grinned and opened the bag.

"Well, you still owe me your company while I eat."

He raised his eyebrows. "Really? You think so?"

"Definitely. I'll feel gypped if I'm forced to eat alone."

He nodded and turned his truck toward the outskirts of town. It looked like we would be ending our night with a game of pool.

*   *   *

"With Sawyer back in town, I didn't expect to see you walking back in here with her," Honey Vincent said when Beau and I walked into the bar.

"I'm entertaining her for Sawyer, Mom. Leave it alone."

Her eyebrows shot up and she glanced back at me. "So Sawyer's okay with you hanging out with Beau, huh? Well, I'll be damned. I was sure he'd have a shit fit once he found out about the two of ya running around town together."

"Beau and I've been friends for as long as Sawyer and I've been. Sawyer is glad we're rekindling our friendship," I explained before Beau could say something snide.

"I'm bettin' he ain't got a clue you're slumming it at a bar with Beau. If he finds out that Beau drags you out here, then he ain't gonna be none too happy about the two of you hangin' out."

"Stay out of it, Mama. We're here to play pool."

I let Beau pull me away from Honey before the two of them got into an argument over whether or not Sawyer would approve of me being here. I was almost positive he would be against it, but it had become my and Beau's thing. I wasn't willing to give this up too. I glanced back at Honey as Beau led me to the pool table. The disapproval in her eyes was obvious. She studied me for a moment before shaking her head and turning to walk back to the bar.

"Sorry about her. She has warmed up to you some, but she still isn't crazy about Sawyer's family, and you being Sawyer's girlfriend makes you a part of it."

I understood the unsaid words. Staying with Sawyer and not chosing Beau over Sawyer had been a mark against me. In her eyes, I was betraying her and Beau.

"That's okay. I get it," I assured Beau, and picked up my cue stick.

"All right, Ash, it's time for me to kick your hot little ass."

"In your dreams, buddy," I replied, knowing good and well he would beat me. I'd gotten better, but not good enough to beat Beau.

Two games later I got a text message from Sawyer.

Sawyer: Are you at home?

I slowly lifted my eyes to meet Beau's. "It's Sawyer asking if I'm at home."

Beau put his cue stick up and reached for mine.

"Tell him I'm taking you home now."

I didn't want to go home right then, but there was no other explanation I could give Sawyer.

I texted him back.

"Beau's taking me home now."

Beau nodded toward the door. "Come on, let's go."

He didn't reach for my hand or touch my back the way he used to when we left the bar. Instead he walked beside me, not touching me or looking at me.

I got another text message.

Sawyer: Tell him to bring you to my house.
Everyone's in bed, and I'm in the pool house.
Come see me. I'll take you home.

That wasn't something I could ask Beau to do. He'd been wonderful after our fight tonight. Asking him to drop me off at Sawyer's was too much.

Once we were in the truck, I fiddled with my phone, trying to decide what to tell Sawyer.

"What is it, Ash? What did he say to make you start chewing your bottom lip?"

I sighed and kept my eyes on the phone in my lap. "He wants you to bring me to his pool house. I don't want you to do that."

Beau pulled the truck off the side of the road and then turned to look at me. "Why?"

I glanced up at him. "Because," I replied.

Beau let out a growl and slammed his palms against the steering wheel, causing me to jump.

"I can't do this, Ash. It's killing me. Having you this close and not touching you is driving me insane. You're his, Ash. You're his. You made your choice, and I understand why you chose him. I don't hold it against you, but dammit, Ash, it hurts."

My chest felt as if it had been ripped open again.

"I'm so sorry, Beau. I'm sorry I did this to you. I'm sorry for everything. I'm sorry I can't make it better. I'm sorry."

"Stop it, Ash. You got nothing to be sorry for. I started this, and I'm the one who needs to end it. I just can't seem to bring myself to stay away from you."

I slid over and straddled the stick shift and laid my head on his shoulder.

He slipped his arm around me and pulled me tight up against him. I closed my eyes as he kissed the top of my head. Neither of us knew what to say. We sat in silence, holding each other until my phone alerted us of another text message. I started to pull away, but Beau held me against his side and cranked the truck.

"Just let me hold you a little longer," he whispered hoarsely as he pulled back onto the road.

When we pulled onto Sawyer's street, Beau kissed my head one more time. "You better move over now."

Chapter 16

ASHTON

Lana was perched on the edge of my bed, flipping through my photo album from last summer when I finally made it home. I closed the door to my room a little harder than needed, unable to hide my frustration that she'd been going through my things again. Her head snapped up in surprise. *Good, I hope I scared her. Serves her right for going through my stuff.*

"Oh. Hey, Ash, you're finally home," she replied, smiling politely.

This girl was not real. She was always soft-spoken, and she never showed any emotion. It was as if my aunt Caroline had given birth to a freaking robot. My mood was crummy, and seeing her infiltrating my personal space didn't make it better.

"I hope you don't mind that I pulled out your photo albums.

Our mothers have been talking in hushed whispers, and I got bored. I'm really glad you're here now."

There was a genuine smile on her face and it made me feel a tad bit guilty for being so aggravated with her. I mean, her dad was a douche bag and her mother wasn't exactly trying to comfort her. Instead she was making everyone in the house relive the experience over and over. Sympathy for what she must be going through won out over my aggravation, and I walked over and sat down next to her.

"Sorry I left you here with them so long. I ended up hanging out at Sawyer's later than I intended." This wasn't exactly true, but that was all she needed to know. A dreamy smile lit her face and she dropped her gaze back to the album in her lap. I glanced down and saw she had opened it to a picture of Sawyer on the beach. His suntanned chest was glistening with water, and he had the silly grin on his face that always reminded me of when we were kids.

"You're so lucky, Ash. Sawyer has to be the most beautiful guy in the world. I remember wishing I could switch places with you when we were kids because you got to play with him and his cousin all the time. Even back then he was so chivalrous and handsome."

Chivalrous and handsome? Who uses those words to describe boys? My mom maybe. I shook my head and flopped down on the bed.

"He's not perfect," I replied, shocking myself. For the first time in my life, I'd admitted Sawyer Vincent had flaws. Lana turned her head to look back at me. Both of her auburn eyebrows were raised up in question.

"No one is perfect, Lana."

She seemed to think about it for a moment then turned to study my album some more.

"I guess that's true. Once I use to think my daddy was perfect. . . ." She trailed off. My heart twisted a little at the hurt sound in her voice. I didn't know if she wanted to talk about it or forget it. Since her mother yapped about it all the time, I would think she'd want to forget.

"The other cousin. What was his name? Bill or Ben?"

"Beau," I replied, curious as to what she was going to say.

"That's right. Ugh, I remember the time Beau handcuffed me to the chain-link fence where Sawyer's daddy kept his hunting dogs. I was terrified of being so close to the gate. I remember thinking that those snarling dogs were going to somehow gnaw my hand off through the fence."

I chuckled at the memory, and Lana twirled around on the bed and frowned at me.

"It isn't funny. You know I'm scared silly of dogs. And that awful boy made me sing 'I'm a Little Teapot' at the top of my lungs, over and over. Each time, he told me to sing it louder if I wanted to get free. And the louder I got, the angrier the dogs got. It was horrible." She stopped, and a soft smile touched her lips, erasing the previous frown. "Then Sawyer showed up, scolded Beau, and unhandcuffed me. You finally popped up out of nowhere about that time and made up some lame excuse about needing Beau's help with something. The two of you took off running with your giggles trailing behind y'all. Sawyer just shook his head as he watched y'all take off and apologized for his cousin. He was so sweet."

I'd forgotten that escapade. We had had so many that I couldn't remember them all. But hearing Lana retell it, I laughed out loud. I'd been hiding behind the big ole oak tree just a few feet away. Beau had told me to stay out of sight in case Sawyer showed up. I'd had to shove my fist in my mouth to keep from laughing out loud at the sound of Lana singing so loudly and off-key.

"I was so sure the two of you would end up together. You're still laughing about my torment seven years later. You two were evil."

I leaned on my elbows and smiled at Lana. "If I remember correctly, you had told me I was as smelly and stinky as an old fish and no boy would ever want to marry me 'cause I stunk and my hair was always as stringy as a mangy dogs."

Lana blushed and covered her mouth. She'd obviously forgotten that part.

"I did, didn't I?" she replied, looking mortified.

I nodded and bit back another laugh at the expression on her face.

"Yep, you did. Beau didn't like it too much, so he decided he'd make you pay for saying something so mean to me. That's the reason he handcuffed you and made you sing."

Lana gave me a knowing smile, "You were hiding behind the tree you came running from when Sawyer showed up, weren't you? The whole time I was being tortured, you were listening."

I laid back down, slipping my hands behind my head.

"Yep, I heard it all."

A pillow hit my head, startling me, and I reached for the one beside me to take a swing at my giggling cousin. *Who knew Lana could be silly?*

"Girls?" My mother's voice interrupted us, and we froze, pillows held high in the air and ready to pummel each other. Mom hesitated before stepping inside the doorway. She'd pulled her blond hair back in a ponytail, and her face was washed clean of makeup. I could see the stress and worry in her eyes. This mess with my aunt was emotionally draining her.

"Yes, ma'am," Lana replied, immediately dropping her pillow like she had been caught doing something horribly wrong. Mom shifted her gaze between the two of us. A smile touched her lips when it became apparent we were having fun not actually fighting.

"Sorry to interrupt the pillow fight," she said, "but I need to speak with Ashton alone for a few minutes if it's okay, Lana." Lana immediately nodded and scurried toward the door. "Thank you," Mom said as she passed, and Lana mumbled something as she kept her head down. It occurred to me that Lana thought I was getting in trouble, and I wanted to laugh. The girl was paranoid.

I threw the pillow back at my bed and sank down onto the large, soft, purple chair beside me.

"What's up?" I asked. Mom took a seat on the edge of my bed, sitting almost exactly like Lana had been. Her back was straight and her hands were folded in her lap. I never realized how different from my mom I really was.

"I need you to do me a favor. Actually, it's a favor for Lana. Tomorrow night your uncle Nolan will be here to talk things out with your aunt Caroline while your father and I referee. We all believe it will be better if Lana isn't here to witness what is said. I am sure at times it's going to be loud and emotional. She's already been through so much. I see no reason to force her to be exposed to this drama. Your father and I want to protect her, and if you could take her out with you tomorrow night, it would be wonderful. I've not forced her upon you since school just started back and you were away from Sawyer most of the summer, but I need your help now."

I agreed that there was no way Lana could be around for the screaming that was bound to come out of the gathering the following night, but I'd already planned on going to the field party with Sawyer. Maybe taking Lana wouldn't be so bad. I'd have more chances to sneak glances at Beau with Lana around. I could distance myself some from Sawyer, using my need to make her comfortable as an excuse.

"Sure. No problem. I'll keep her out late."

It was at least an hour later before Lana returned to my room. The solitude had been nice. I'd checked my e-mails. Responded to one from Leann. Then I'd curled up on my bed and listened to my favorite playlist. When Lana quietly stepped into my room, she was already in her pajamas and her hair hung in thick wet locks framing her pale face. I'd always envied her pretty red hair. Her pale skin and freckles I could do without, but her hair I envied. Reaching up, I pulled the earbuds from my ear.

"Hey," she said, walking over to the twin mattress on the floor beside my bed.

"Hey," I replied, wondering what had put the sad expression on her face. Knowing my aunt, she had told Lana about her dad coming tomorrow night. The woman was as dumb as a box of rocks. How she was blood-related to my mother was beyond me.

"You okay?" I asked as she pulled back the quilt on her mattress and slipped under the covers. She shrugged her shoulders, then turned her head to peer up at me.

"I know he's coming."

I nodded.

"Thanks for taking me out. I don't think I'm ready to see him."

In a way, I could understand. He'd not only betrayed her mother; he'd betrayed her, too. I'd be furious with my dad for doing something like that. But then, it wouldn't make me stop loving him and missing him. Lana hadn't seen her dad in more than a week. Surely she missed him. Even a little.

"Will you ever be ready to see him?" I asked, wondering if I should just keep my mouth shut. She didn't respond right away, and I was beginning to think she wasn't going to.

"Someday. Just not yet," she whispered against the quilt touching her chin.

I lay down on my pillow and stared up at the ceiling. My parents might drive me crazy with their need for me to be perfect, but at least they'd never put me through the pain I knew Lana must be experiencing.

Chapter 17

BEAU

I decided to completely end things with Nicole. She wasn't taking it well, but Nicole wasn't used to rejection. I stepped into the clearing, and the familiar smell of burning pecan wood and loud music greeted me. I heard my name shouted a few times in greeting, but I didn't pay attention to who it was. I wasn't here tonight to socialize. I'd come for one reason. There were other things I could have done tonight. But other things didn't include getting a glimpse of Ashton. My world revolved around seeing her. If I knew she was going to be somewhere, I went. It had gotten to the point where I was considering going to church on Sunday. I knew from hearing Sawyer talk about it, Ash sang solos most Sundays for the choir. I hadn't heard her sweet voice in years.

"Is it true? Did you really break things off with Nicole?" I turned to see Kyle Jacobson walking up beside me, grinning. He'd always had a thing for Nicole. I was about to make his night.

"Yep," I replied, reaching for a Solo cup and filling it up with cold beer from the keg.

"So is she fair game, or are you going to bust a guy up if he goes after her?"

I took a swig of the beer and chuckled. I'd actually pay someone to get her off my back. The moment she realized I'd ditched her because I was in love with Ashton, her claws were going to come out. I couldn't let her hurt Ash.

"Man, she's a free bird. Please be my guest."

Kyle slapped me on the back. "Hot damn."

If he only knew. The girl had issues a mile long. I nodded and continued to drink my beer, scanning the crowd for any sign of Ash.

The moment she stepped into the clearing holding Sawyer's hand my heart sped up. Just seeing her made me a little crazy. I hated seeing her hand tucked in Sawyer's, but she wasn't paying any attention to Sawyer. She was searching the crowd, for me. I threw my cup in the trash can and made my way over to them. Once I stepped out of the shadows, her eyes found mine and a pleased smile lifted the corners of her mouth. Desire curled in my gut, making it hard not to go jerk her away from Sawyer and claim her as mine. He shouldn't be touching her.

"Sawyer," I said, nodding to my cousin before allowing myself to stare at Ashton some more. The tight jeans she wore clung to her hips, while her flat, tanned stomach played peek-a-boo with the hem of her pale blue tank top. I knew exactly how soft that little strip of skin felt against my fingers. I lifted my eyes from her stomach to meet her gaze. "Ash." I watched her blush prettily, then duck her head and glance over through her lowered lashes at the person standing beside her. I followed her gaze and saw who could only be a grown-up version of Lana. She smiled at me, but I could see it was forced. It took all my restraint to hold back a chuckle. I'd tormented the girl when we were kids, but she had always been so mean to Ash.

"Beau, you remember Lana. I believe you once handcuffed her to the dog fence and forced her to sing loudly for her release."

Ashton's introduction made me laugh. I couldn't stop myself this time. I remember seeing Ashton's head full of blond curls peeking at me from around the tree trunk, covering her mouth as her shoulders shook from laughter. I'd been so proud of myself for avenging her honor and making her laugh all at the same time. I met Ashton's amused gaze, wishing for the millionth time that things had gone differently and she was mine.

"I remember that. You tormented Lana so much, it's a wonder she didn't run screaming when she saw you tonight."

Sawyer's voice startled me. I'd forgotten he was standing there. I couldn't think of much else with Ashton smiling up at me so sweetly.

I cleared my throat and turned my attention to Lana. "Ah, yes, but I believe you asked for it. You use to say some pretty harsh things to Ash, and I never let anyone talk to her that way."

Lana gave me a smile that said she knew more than she should. Had Ashton told her cousin about us? The idea she'd told someone about our summer together made me happier than it should. I wanted her to think about it. I wanted her to need to tell someone. Hell, I just wanted her.

"Where's Nicole?" Sawyer asked, glancing over my shoulder as if expecting Nicole to latch on to me at any moment.

It took all my willpower not to look at Ashton when I replied, "I broke it off with Nic. Don't care where she is." I wanted to see Ashton's expression.

"Huh, really? I wasn't expecting that. She isn't pregnant, is she?" Sawyer's accusation that I'd broken up with Nicole because I'd knocked her up grated on my nerves. Had he always assumed the worst of me?

"No. It's just over," I replied in a harder tone than I usually used with him.

"Is there someone else?" Sawyer asked.

I wondered how he would react if I told him his girlfriend was the someone else. No doubt I'd lose him forever. His arm snaked around Ashton's waist. Right then it was hard to remember he was my cousin. All I could focus on was the intense desire to rip the arm he was touching Ashton with off his body.

"Why don't we go join the group over there and stop giving Beau the third degree?" This time I couldn't help but look at Ashton. A smile touched her lips before she turned away from me and gazed up at Sawyer.

"You're right, baby. I can grill him some other time," Sawyer replied, and winked at me before leading Ashton toward the group.

I stood there, unable to follow them. Seeing her cuddled up against his side was painful. Breaking up with Nic had been the fair thing to do since I was using her only to cope, but now there was no distraction to keep me from watching Sawyer with Ash.

"This may not be my business, but the way you and Ashton keep staring at each other like you want to take a bite is going to eventually tip your cousin off. He's a trusting person, but I don't think he's stupid."

I jerked my gaze off of Ashton and Sawyer's retreating forms, and turned to see Lana still standing there, frowning at me with her hands on her hips. What did she know?

"You're right—it isn't your business," I snapped, and started toward the keg. I needed another drink.

* * *

ASHTON

Sawyer was going out of his way to make sure Lana felt comfortable with everyone. He had introduced her to the core of his friends and had even gone to get her a soda. It didn't bother me. In fact, it gave me time to watch Beau without distraction. Not having Nicole wrapped around him was a relief, but it also made it almost impossible to take my eyes off him. Beau caught me staring and winked. I bit my bottom lip to keep from laughing. A sharp elbow nudged me in the ribs, causing me to gasp and spin around to find the person who belonged to the bony arm. Lana was smiling innocently at me.

"You're being obvious," she hissed, keeping a fake smile on her face. Her meaning, however, sunk in.

"I need to go to the car and get my phone. My mom's probably called me ten times by now," Lana announced.

"I'll go with you," I quickly replied, glancing up at Sawyer, who seemed pleased I was being nice to my cousin. I used to seek out this sort of approval from him, but now it annoyed me. If I didn't like my cousin, I'd stomp on her foot just to piss him off.

Once we were safely out of the clearing and headed for the car, Lana stopped walking and turned to glare at me. "You've about ten minutes or so to get yourself together before your knight in shining armor comes looking for us. I'm going to go get my phone and make a few calls."

I frowned. "What do you mean?"

"I mean you need to stop openly flirting with Beau while the entire football team is around to witness it. It's like you two think you're the only ones out there. We all have eyes, you know."

She spun around and headed deeper into the pecan orchard and toward the parked cars.

"She's got a point, but it's my fault." Beau's voice should have startled me, but it didn't. Somehow I knew he'd find a way to get me alone.

"Yes, it probably is," I said teasingly as I turned around to meet his gaze.

Beau took a step toward me and ran his hand through his hair, muttering a curse.

"I want to rip his damn arms off his body, Ash. Sawyer, who I'd do anything for. I want to hurt him. If he touches you again in front of me, I'm going to crack. I can't take this."

I closed the space between us and wrapped my arms around his waist. I'd done this. My need to be near Beau had created this impossible situation.

"I'm sorry," I whispered against his chest, wishing I could make it all go away. He sighed and wrapped his arms around me, pulling me tighter up against him.

"Don't be sorry. Just try not to let him touch you. When he touches you, I see red. I can't take it. I don't want to see him or anyone else touch you."

I pulled back just enough so I could gaze up at him. His jaw was clenched tightly. Knowing he was thinking of Sawyer with such ferocity made me feel so guilty. I hadn't wanted to come between them, yet I was doing it anyway.

"What can I do to make this right, Beau? I don't want to come between y'all. It's the main reason I'm doing this. He's your family."

Beau slipped his fingers into my hair and cradled my head.

"Staying with him. Letting him touch you, hold you, God. It's eating me alive. You may be keeping Sawyer from hating me, but you're only making me hate him."

I reached up and clasped his hands, pulling them away from my head as I stepped back. Tears blurred my vision. "What am I supposed to do, Beau? You tell me. What am I supposed to do?"

He opened his mouth to respond and closed it as his eyes settled on something over my left shoulder. A possessive gleam came into his eyes as if to warn off any predators that might get near what was his. I knew without turning around who he was glowering at so fiercely. I didn't glance back at Sawyer. I wasn't sure what to say.

"What's going on? Ashton never yells at people. What in the crap did you do to her, Beau?"

"It's my fault." Lana's voice had me snapping my head up from my defeated stance as I turned to gawk at her.

"What?" Beau and Sawyer said at the same time.

Lana gave us all a dramatic sigh and shrugged her shoulders.

"Beau was flirting with me and Ash didn't like it. She thinks he isn't good enough for me or something. They started bickering when she told Beau to leave me alone."

I couldn't believe my ears. Had Lana just lied so believably for me and Beau?

She smiled and nibbled on her fingernail like some flirty bimbo and smirked. "What? Might as well tell him the truth. You don't think his cousin is worthy of your cousin."

I tore my gaze off my shy, meek cousin-turned-drama-queen to study Sawyer's face. Was he actually falling for this? Surely not. He was frowning at Beau.

"Beau, leave Ash's cousin alone. She's not one of your one-nighters. Go find some other rebound girl. There's no use getting Ash all worked up over this."

Unbelievable.

I glanced over at Beau, and his expression told me he was past furious. He was ready to kill Sawyer. I stepped in between them, putting my back to Sawyer and silently pleading with Beau. I mouthed the word "please" and watched the anger ease some before he turned and stalked off deeper into the pecan orchard.

I needed to make sure he was okay, but I couldn't do that with Sawyer standing behind me, waiting for me to return to the field with him. Back to playing pretend. Back to being miserable.

Chapter 18

ASHTON

As we stepped into my bedroom, I reached for the light switch. Lana walked around me and dropped her purse on my dresser, then leveled me with a frown. She hadn't said anything on the ride home. I'd been forced to carry on a conversation with Sawyer as if nothing had happened while she sat silently in the back. Apparently, she was ready to talk.

"I did that for you tonight not because I think what you're doing is right or wrong, but because I think you needed a wake-up call, not a crucifixion." I raised my eyebrows at her explanation. "Sawyer's a good guy. He and Beau have always been close. I can remember how thick as thieves you three were as kids. I envied your friendship with those boys. Y'all had something special. Something unique. I couldn't just stand there and let it all come crumbling down. Besides, from the look on Beau's face I'm afraid he would have killed Sawyer with his bare hands had Sawyer said the wrong thing."

I sank down onto my bed and buried my head in my hands. This was a disaster. She was right. I was ruining a lifetime friendship. "What do I do?" I asked, knowing she didn't have the magical answer either. Lana sat down beside me and patted my back, which made me feel even worse. Here I was having a breakdown over two guys, and she'd been out with me tonight because her cheating father had come to face her obnoxious mother. In the grand scheme of things, her problems were much bigger.

"You choose one and let the other one go."

It sounded incredibly simple, yet it was impossible. Didn't she see that?

"I can't. No matter who I choose, one of them will hate the other and possibly me. Choosing one of them won't fix anything."

"You're right. It won't. You need to let them both go. If you let them both go, then one day you all will have a chance of finding the friendship that this is destroying."

I hated that her words made sense. I needed to break up with Sawyer, and we all needed to move on. My chest constricted at the thought of walking away from Beau, of not having his arms around me or burying my face in his chest. But I couldn't have him. Having him would eventually mean losing him. He'd never get over losing Sawyer. Me, he could live without. A hot tear rolled off my chin, and I reached up to wipe it away. I'd made this mess. It was only right I fix it.

"You're right," I whispered, staring straight ahead, "but I wish you weren't."

A soft knock on the door reminded me of the other issues going on in the house tonight. I reached over and squeezed Lana's hand before the door opened and her mother stepped inside. Her hair was the same color as mine and my mother's, but that was as far as the family resemblance went. Where my mother was thin and petite, my aunt was heavy and big-boned and she wore a permanent scowl. She never seemed happy, even before she'd caught her husband cheating on her. She hadn't been here when we got home. Mom and Dad had also been missing. From the sounds coming down the hall, everyone was back.

"Hey, girls. Um, Lana, sweetheart, let's go talk a little bit, okay?"

Lana's hand squeezed mine this time before she stood up. If my aunt would let me, I'd go with her and hold her hand through the whole conversation. Lana had ended up being the friend I so desperately needed this past week. My door closed behind them, and I lay back on my bed and whispered a little prayer for Lana. *God knows she needs it with a mama like hers.*

*   *   *

I was growing weary of good-byes. Lana and her mother stood at our front door with their suitcases in hand. My aunt was headed back home to take my uncle to the cleaners in what would be an ugly divorce. Lana had a lot of drama and pain ahead of her. I'd begged her to just stay here with us. She could let her parents battle it out without her around, but she said her mother needed her right now. In a way I understood, but then I wondered, *If I had been in Lana's shoes, would I be so kind?* She was really the better person. I was the selfish brat.

"I'm going to miss you," I said, wishing my voice didn't sound so forlorn. Strange how you can think someone is ruining your life and they end up being your friend. I'd been so upset over having to share my space and listen to my aunt that I hadn't realized I had a friend right under my nose when I needed one the most. I still needed her.

"I'm going to miss you, too. Keep me updated on your . . . life," she said with a small lift of her eyebrows.

I nodded, then leaned in to hug her. "Thank you," I whispered in her ear.

"You're welcome," she whispered back.

"I'm so glad you girls have bonded again after all these years," my aunt said. "We'll have to come back and visit again soon—after I get through the divorce and all. Maybe I can use my extra money to take the two of you on a cruise. Wouldn't that be fun?" There was no way I was going on a trip with that crazy woman, much less on a ship where it would be impossible to run away from her. The smirk on Lana's face had me forcing back a giggle. She knew well and good there was no way I was going on a trip with her mama.

"All right, y'all, we'll be in touch," my aunt said brightly, and turned to head out to her Lincoln Town Car. I stood watching as my dad helped them load their luggage into the trunk and my mother hugged and talked to her sister. Lana waved at me from the passenger seat. My room would be quiet and all mine again . . . but that no longer sounded appealing.

There are some things you don't expect to see, and Beau Vincent sauntering into church on a Sunday morning is one of them. Finishing my solo hadn't been easy. My eyes wanted to eat him up as he sat alone on the back pew, wearing jeans and a snug, navy blue polo that stretched across his broad chest.

Sawyer hadn't noticed his cousin because he was in the third row to the front. I'd been sitting in that row since I was a little girl. My parents expected me to sit in either the first, second, or third pew. I couldn't go back any farther. Sawyer never complained. Every Sunday he was right there waiting on me to finish singing in the choir.

My gaze drifted back to meet Beau's even though I knew it was a bad idea. He was liable to make me forget the words. A slow, titillating grin touched his lips. It suddenly felt like it was a hundred degrees in the sanctuary. My face flushed, and I tore my eyes off him and his delectable mouth. Somehow I managed to finish the words to "How Great Thou Art" without messing up. The choir began to exit through the side doors of the stage, and normally, I just made my way down to my pew. Today, however, I needed a breather. I fell in behind Mary Hill and let out a sigh of relief as I stepped into the warm sunshine.

"You leaving?" Jason Tibbs asked, sticking his pimply face out the door and frowning at me. His dad was the associate pastor, so he felt our meager relationship gave him the right to question my actions. Instead of insulting him, I took a deep breath, forced a smile, and glanced back at him.

"No, my head is hurting. I needed to take a quiet break."

He grinned, showing way too much gum and flashing his crooked overbite. His dad really needed to send the boy to a dermatologist and an orthodontist.

"Okay, I'll leave the door unlocked so you don't have to walk all the way around the building to get back inside."

I nodded and said an obligatory "Thanks."

The door closed quietly behind him, and I knew I had limited time before people started to notice that I was missing from the third row.

"You hiding out here because of me?"

Beau's voice caused me to gasp. His long legs ate up the

grass as he closed the distance between us. I couldn't keep from ogling him. It was just unfair for someone to look that good in a pair of Levis.

"No response means yes," he said with a smirk on his face as he came to a stop mere inches from me. He knew I was lusting, and he liked it. Determined to regain some of my dignity, I straightened my posture and flipped my hair over my shoulders as I peered up at him.

"I always come out here to get some fresh air before I go sit down for an hour of preaching," I lied.

Beau chuckled and reached out to trace a line from my ear to my lips. "Why don't I believe you?" he asked. His voice deepened as he studied my mouth. All I could manage was a shrug. His thumb was delicately brushing over my bottom lip as if he were asking for admittance and I was lost. We were standing right outside the church where anyone could walk out and catch us, but all I could think about was pressing my lips against his. Beau was becoming a necessity, and nothing about such a revelation could be considered positive.

"Beau, what are you doing?" I croaked out.

"Yeah, Beau, I'd like to know the same thing," said a voice that didn't belong to Beau.

Several things happened at once. Beau's thumb stopped its caressing, but he didn't drop his hand. I could feel his body tense at the sound of Sawyer's voice. What I should have done and what I did do were in two different stratospheres. Stepping back and putting distance between Beau and me would have been the logical, intelligent thing to do. Reaching out and grabbing his arm and squeezing it was my immediate reaction.

"Are either of you gonna speak or are you just gonna continue gawking at each other?"

The hard edge to Sawyer's voice woke me up out of the trance I'd been in, and I dropped my hand from Beau and took several steps back. If Sawyer was expected to keep his cool, then we needed to put some space between the two of us. Beau's eyes bore into me. He was silently pleading with me. I could almost hear his thoughts. Then he turned to face his cousin. This was the confrontation I'd hoped would never happen.

"What exactly are you insinuating, Sawyer?" Beau asked in a deadly calm tone I knew he'd never used with Sawyer.

"Oh, I don't know, cuz, maybe the fact I came out here to look for my girlfriend, and I found her being mauled by you."

Beau took a step forward and a low growl rumbled in his chest. I ran up and grabbed his arm with both my hands. This probably didn't help Sawyer's temper any, but it kept Beau from pummeling his face. Both boys were in shape, but Beau had the market on badass. I couldn't let him do something he'd never forgive himself for.

Sawyer stared fixedly at me. I could only imagine what was going through his head. The sad thing was that I knew he wouldn't even get close to the truth. Sawyer would never imagine I'd lost my virginity to Beau in the bed of a truck.

"Want to tell me what's going on, Ash?" There was hurt in his voice. I hated knowing that the words I had to say to him wouldn't erase this but would only make it worse. I pushed Beau behind me as I stepped in front of him.

"Go on home, Beau. Sawyer and I need to talk, and I don't want you here." Turning back to see Beau's reaction was tempting, but I didn't do it. I kept my eyes on Sawyer, praying silently that Beau heeded my orders and left. It was time I finished this and saved their friendship before it was too late.

"I don't want to leave you alone," he replied, steel lacing his words.

"Beau, please. You aren't helping matters. Just go."

Sawyer never took his eyes off me. He was trying so hard to read between the lines. I would have to tell him some truths— just enough to keep from destroying his relationship with Beau.

The crunch of the dry grass under Beau's boots told me he'd granted my wish and was heading for his truck. I'd won that battle. Now the biggest one was staring me in the face, and I had no idea what I was going to say.

Chapter 19

ASHTON

"Start at the beginning, Ash, and tell me everything."

There was no way I'd tell him everything. I stared out at the road as Beau's truck drove away. The silence was deafening as Sawyer waited for me to speak.

"This summer, Beau and I rekindled our friendship. We were close once, Sawyer, you know that." I paused and took a deep breath. "He understands me. He knows when I'm full of bullcrap and he knows I'm not perfect even though I try really hard to be. With Beau, I can let myself go and not worry about losing his friendship."

"So this is a friends' thing? Because the way he was caressing your mouth and eating you up with his eyes, I find that a little hard to believe."

"All it can ever be with Beau is friendship. He knows that. Beau is affectionate. He touches a lot of girls' lips."

Sawyer raised his eyebrows as if he thought what I was saying was ludicrous. "I don't know if we're talking about the same guy, but Beau, my cousin Beau, doesn't longingly gaze at anyone the way I just caught him staring at you. You're too naive to see it, but trust me, baby, he wants you, and I'm going to kick his ass."

Okay, that wasn't what I'd been aiming for: blame on Beau, not me. I needed to redirect this anger of his.

"You misunderstood what you saw. He was trying to talk me out of what I'd decided to do today. He believes you and I are supposed to be forever. I don't think so. We're young and I need space. I'm not ready to talk about marrying you one day. That scares me. There is so much life out there to live first. Beau thinks I'm making a mistake because he thinks you're the best thing that has ever happened to me. What you saw was your cousin trying to persuade me not to break up with you."

The look of disbelief and shock that came over Sawyer's face was a little insulting. Why was it so hard for him to believe I'd break up with him?

"You—you're . . . breaking up with me?" He shook his head and stepped back, away from me. His face had gone pale, as if I'd just told him he'd never play football again. This wasn't the end of the world.

"I pretend with you, Sawyer. I'm not the good girl you think I am. You love this fake Ashton. I've been striving to be worthy of you for so long, and I'm exhausted. I don't like returning the stupid buggies to the return place in the parking lot, and I don't like feeling as if I have to be Good Samaritan to everyone I come across. Sometimes I just want to run off and worry about me. I'm selfish and ornery and just a big ole fake. This girl you love and want to marry doesn't exist."

It was as if a weight had just been lifted off my shoulders. The air rushed into my lungs, and for the first time in three years I took a deep breath.

"That's crazy," Sawyer said, shaking his head. I was so close to freedom then that I could taste it. Standing here and listening to him try to convince me I didn't know what I was talking about annoyed me. But I could control this now. The real Ashton had a backbone.

"No, it's the truth. I want to go parking and make out so heavy my bra gets lost under the seat of the car. I want to flip Nicole the bird when she glares at me in the hallways at school. And I want to wear my red bikini and enjoy the fact guys are checking me out. I'm not who you think I am. I never was and I never will be."

I closed the space between us, stood on my tippy-toes, and placed a quick peck on his cheek. The familiar smell of his cologne caused my chest to tighten with emotion. I'd miss him, but not enough to be someone else to have him. He saw me differently now. I could see it in his expression. The emotion churning in his blue eyes as he finally saw me for who I really was was bittersweet. I spun around and jogged out to my Jetta. Without another glance back, I drove off. For the first time ever, I left church before it was over.

When I pulled into the parking lot, Leann was sitting on the front steps of the ancient, three-story brick dormitory she'd been placed in that year. From where I was, I could see her nibbling on her thumbnail. Leann mauled her right thumbnail only when she was nervous. I'd been vague on my reason for coming when I'd called after I'd decided that was where I was going to go. I swooped into an empty parking spot. On my drive up there, I realized that telling someone everything had become essential. I needed to get this off my chest. A tap on my window startled me, and I glanced over to see Leann, still nibbling her thumbnail, with a frown puckering her brow. Forcing a smile, I opened the door. She stepped back so I could get out.

"I swear I think I grew gray hair waiting on you to get here," she said, reaching for my arm and pulling me into a hug. "I can't believe you're here, and I can't believe you left church early without telling anyone where you were going."

I pulled back and meet her gaze. "I didn't tell you that."

She rolled her big brown eyes and hooked her arm through

mine, steering me toward the dorm. "Sweetie, the moment it was apparent you weren't returning to the church service, I received texts from my aunt Linda and Kayla, and then Kyle posted it on his Facebook wall."

I groaned and laid my head on her shoulder. Leann patted my arm and led me over to sit at a secluded bench in the shade of a large oak tree. Plopping down, she patted the empty spot beside her. "Come on and spill it. The suspense is killing me. Never have you been the cause of gossip. This has got to be good."

I shifted on the wooden seat and studied my hands in my lap. Admitting this was one thing; actually looking Leann in the face while I shared all my faults with her was another. We'd been friends for three years, and not one time had I ever mentioned even a mild attraction to Beau.

"You know Beau and I were close as kids. . . ." I decided to start there. It seemed like the best place.

"Oh good God, you mean to tell me this has something to do with Beau? Beau Vincent?" I cringed and nodded without glancing over at her.

"Yes, it has everything to do with Beau," I whispered.

Leann's hand covered mine, and I took some comfort in the gesture.

"This summer Beau and I started spending time together. You were with Noah or working, and Sawyer was gone. I thought it would be good to rekindle the friendship Beau and I once shared."

Leann squeezed my hands, and I continued to explain how we'd played pool at the bar where his mother worked, went swimming at the hole, watched a movie at my house, and then I paused, knowing what I told her next was going to be hard for her to comprehend. After all, I was the good girl.

"That night in the back of his truck, Beau and I . . . we"—I swallowed hard and squeezed my eyes shut—"had sex."

Leann let go of my hands and slipped her arm around my shoulders instead.

"Wow" was her only response.

"I know. It wasn't the only time either and . . . and although I know it won't happen again . . . I think . . . I think I love him. Maybe I always have. No. I know I always have. When I'm with Beau, I feel things I've never felt with Sawyer. I can be me. There's no pretending. Beau knows my worst flaws."

"The heart wants who the heart wants. We can't help that," Leann said.

I sighed and finally lifted my eyes to meet hers. The unshed tears blurred my vision.

"But I've ruined his life. All he ever had was Sawyer. Make no mistake, I went after Beau. I can look back and see it now. This is all my fault. I should have never come between them." I sniffled and buried my head in her shoulder.

"Beau could have said no. He knew he was destroying his relationship with Sawyer every moment he spent with you. Don't you take all the blame for this." The stern tone in Leann's voice only caused me to cry harder. Beau needed Sawyer. He might not have realized it, but he did. Somehow I had to make it right.

"How do I fix this? How do I help Beau get Sawyer back?"

"You can't fix this for them. Beau knew what he was doing, Ash. He chose you over Sawyer. Now that you've let Sawyer go, are you going to choose Beau?"

I wiped the tears from my cheeks and peered over at her. "Choosing Beau will cause everyone in Grove to hate him. They'll all see him as the guy who took Sawyer's girl away. I can't do that to him."

Leann shrugged. "I don't think Beau cares about everyone else. He made that apparent when he decided sneaking around with his cousin's girl was what he wanted to do. He has to love you, Ash. Never in this lifetime would I have thought Beau would do anything to hurt Sawyer. He loves him. So that can only mean he loves you more." She reached over to pat my shoulder. "Question is: Do you love him as fiercely? Are you willing to snub your nose at your family and the people in town in order to have him?"

Chapter 20

BEAU

"Well, Hell has done froze slap over. Sawyer Vincent is walking into a bar." My mama's voice carried loud and clear over the empty room. I put the beer down that I'd been nursing since walking in there five minutes before. Ashton was nowhere to be found, so I had come here hoping she was looking for me, too.

"I'm not here for a social visit, Aunt Honey. I came to see my backstabbing, lying SOB of a cousin."

Mama let out a low whistle and shook her head. "I shoulda known better than to believe you knew all about Beau and Ashton galavanting around town together."

"Shut up, Mom," I said without glancing her way. I kept my eyes on Sawyer. The hatred in his eyes wasn't something I'd ever imagined seeing directed my way. Even though I knew I deserved it, I still had a hard time swallowing it. His hair was tucked behind his ears and his teeth were so tightly clenched I could see his jaw tick.

"Is she here?" Sawyer asked, scanning the empty bar. He'd thought she would come to me too.

"No."

"Where is she?"

"I don't know."

Sawyer stalked toward me. God, I didn't want to hit him. I just wanted Ash. The real Ash. The one he didn't know. The one he'd never be able to love.

"How could you do this, Beau? You're like my brother."

The pain in his eyes felt like a knife twisting in my gut. It wasn't enough to make me regret anything, but it hurt like hell.

"You don't know her. You never did."

"I don't know her? *I* don't know her? Who in the hell do you think you are, Beau? She's been mine for three years. Three years. The two of you hardly acknowledged each other for those three years. Then I leave for the summer and you two make up? Become friends? What exactly happened? Because the bullcrap she tried to feed me outside the church isn't gonna fly."

Do I tell him the truth? He deserved the truth, but I couldn't tell him everything without Ash's consent. It was her story too.

"We got close. We spent time together. We remembered why we were so close when we were younger." I stopped and stared at him. There was one truth he needed to know, one truth that was mine to tell. But admitting it would probably kill any chance of us ever getting over this. It all boiled down to who was more important. My cousin, the one guy I'd always known would stand by me no matter what, my best friend. Then there was Ash, the one person I couldn't live without, not anymore. "I love her."

Sawyer's jaw dropped, then clenched within a second. He was gearing up to take a swing at me. I could see it in his stance.

"You. Love. Her," he repeated in angry disbelief. "Are you aware that I intend to marry her one day? What about you, Beau, huh? You planning on marrying her? Moving her into your mama's trailer? Maybe she could get a job working here with Aunt Honey once her parents completely cut her off."

My fist slammed into his face before I knew what was happening. Sawyer staggered back, blood trickling down his nose. A loud roar erupted from his chest and he charged at me, tackling me to the ground. His fist connected with my jaw only because I knew I deserved it. But that was the last lick I'd take from him. The blood running down over his mouth from his nose had me doing everything in my power to constrain him. I didn't want to hit him again, but I'd be damned if I'd let him hit me.

"Stop it, both of you!" Mama yelled over our grunts, but Sawyer didn't stop trying to take swings at me and I didn't stop blocking his hits.

"You're a bastard, Beau. She's a good girl. You can't give her what I can." Sawyer's words caused me to temporarily lose my cool, and my fist planted onto the side of his face again. Damn. He needed to shut the hell up.

"Shut up, Saw," I yelled, shoving him off me and standing up.

"It's true and you know it. She's just too stupid to realize it—" He didn't finish his sentence before I had him flat on his back, holding him to the ground with my hand clamped over his throat.

"Don't ever call her stupid again," I warned. He'd crossed a line. I loved him, but I loved her more.

"That's it. Get off him now, Beau," Mama said. "This has gone on long enough. You two are letting a girl ruin your relationship. Neither of y'all are gonna marry her. You're kids. She's sweet and pretty, I'll give y'all that, but she ain't worth throwing away your family for."

Mama stood over us, her shadow covering Sawyer's face. I eased up on my grip around his neck in case he was turning blue and I couldn't tell.

"He isn't my family." Sawyer's words stung, but if he'd taken Ash from me, then I'd feel the same way. I released my choke hold on him and stood up again, putting distance between us. Never taking my eyes off him.

"Sorry, kiddo, but being pissed at him over that girl don't take away the blood running through your veins. Y'all are, and forever will be, family."

Sawyer sneered as he stood up and wiped the blood from his nose onto his shirt sleeve.

"He's just my dad's loser brother's bastard."

I didn't react. He wanted me to, but I didn't. Mama clicked her tongue like she always did when she knew something important no one else did. I let my eyes dart toward her for a second to see what she was up to.

"Actually, Beau ain't your daddy's brother's bastard. He's your daddy's bastard. The blood in his veins is the very same in yours, boy. Make no mistake 'bout that."

Frozen in my spot, I let Mama's words sink in. I stumbled backward and grabbed the edge of the pool table for support as I stared at her, waiting for some sign that she was lying.

"No" was Sawyer's only response.

I couldn't look at him. Not now.

"Yes. Ask your daddy. Hell, ask your mama. That ought to be loads of fun. She hates me anyhow. Might as well make her hate me more for lettin' the cat outta the bag."

She was telling the truth. It was in her voice. I'd heard her lies all my life. I knew how to tell the difference.

"No. You're just a stupid whore. My dad would never."

Mama cackled and walked back around the bar to grab a towel. Then she slung it at Sawyer.

"Wipe the blood off your face and go home. Once you realize I'm telling the truth, you and your brother can work things out. Like I said, ain't no girl worth fighting over. You might want to ask your daddy about that, too. I'm sure he has an opinion on it. Seeing as the apple don't fall far from the tree."

What was she saying? A bitter smile touched her lips.

"I don't know what's worse. Finding out you're white trash after all or having your mama try and foist you off on my dad." Sawyer spat out the words before turning and walking back out the door he'd come barreling through only fifteen minutes before.

ASHTON

"Well, Grana, I'm back. It's time to face the music," I said as I laid the single-stem pink rose on the headstone of Grana's grave the next morning.

I'd gotten up at four that morning, after spending the night with Leann, to make it back in time for school. I didn't need an unexcused absence to add to my list of transgressions. My parents were probably going to ground me for life as it was.

I sat down on the wooden bench at the foot of the grave. My mom had taken the bench from Grana's porch and brought it here.

"I messed up big. You weren't here to run to, so I took off to Leann's, which probably only made things worse. I even left church right after the choir solo. I doubt Mom and Dad know why yet, but I don't think it really matters."

I took a sip of the mocha latte I'd picked up on my way into town. School didn't start for another hour, and going home right now would be bad.

"It's all because of Beau. I love him. Crazy, huh? Beau Vincent, the town bad boy, and I have to love him. Me, the ex-girlfriend of his best friend and cousin. But he lets me be me, Grana. Just like you did. He isn't bad like everyone thinks. No one knows his heart. They can't look past his foul-mouth, beer-drinking, rebellious attitude to see he's just a boy without a dad. No one reached out and tried to teach him any better. He was left alone to grow up. It isn't fair. Everyone judges him even knowing he had no positive influence in his life. His uncle sure didn't try to care for, discipline, or take an interest in him. I think he turned out wonderful despite the bad hand he was dealt. I hate how everyone judges others around here. They call this place the Bible Belt, but really, Grana, I think they all need to go read their Bibles a little more. I distinctly remember Jesus befriending sinners—not judging them. Beau just needs someone to believe in him, and I do."

I took another long gulp of my latte and leaned back on the bench. The church graveyard was quiet in the early-morning hour. A school bus passing was the only sign of life.

My phone dinged, alerting me of a text. I glanced down at it, and frowned.

Sawyer: Where are you and where is Beau?

I hesitated, not sure how to answer. The fact that Beau was missing bothered me, though.

Me: I'm at Grana's grave. I haven't seen Beau since he left church yesterday.

I waited for a reply, but none came. Grabbing my keys from the bench beside me, I stood up.

"I need to go, Grana. Love you," I said, and blew a kiss toward her headstone before making my way back to the car.

Chapter 21

ASHTON

Before I could close my car door, Sawyer was in front of me. He looked like he hadn't slept at all last night, and he had a cut on his nose and a bruise under his right eye.

"What happened—?"

"Where is he?" Sawyer ordered, cutting off my question. I shook my head, staring up at him, trying to figure out why he was so determined to find Beau.

"I told you I don't know. I left church and went to see Leann. I stayed the night at her dorm and came back this morning."

Sawyer mumbled something that sounded like a curse, and my eyes flew open in shock. The sun beamed down on his face, and under the bruise I could see swelling along his right cheekbone. Apparently, he'd found Beau yesterday at some point.

"Did Beau—?" I reached up to touch his face and he swatted my hand away with a disgusted sneer.

"Don't touch me. You made your bed, Ashton, now you can lie in it. I'm not yours to touch."

He was right, of course. I simply nodded. Anger lit up his blue eyes.

"You did this, you know. He's gone because of you. You ruined his life. I hope it was worth it." Sawyer's voice was laced with the anger flashing in his eyes. One thing was for sure: He hated me.

I didn't nod this time. I just stepped around him and walked away. It hurt too bad to see the hatred in his eyes directed at me. I needed to find Beau. Not calling him yesterday had been a bad move, but I had refused to believe he'd run off. He'd been ready to fight for me. And from the battered appearance of Sawyer's face, he did fight for me. I was ready to choose him over everyone else. It was time I threw caution to the wind and went after what I wanted too. And I wanted Beau.

Eight hours later I stood outside, staring at the door of the bar where Honey Vincent worked. I hadn't ever been there in the daylight. The peeling paint and badly beaten-up door weren't noticeable in the dark. Beau hadn't shown up for school today. People who had once spoken to me acted as if I didn't exist. It would have bothered me if I hadn't been so worried about Beau. I'd texted him several times, but there was never a response. Sawyer had directed his angry glare my way only once, when he was heading to the field house after school. He had walked by my locker and shaken his head as if to blame me for his cousin's absence. My fear that he was right had gotten stronger all day long. I should have called Beau yesterday. No, I should have stayed by his side. At the first sign of struggle, I had lied and run, leaving him to hold the bag. *I'm an awful person.*

The door to the bar opened, and Honey stood there with her hand on her hip, staring directly at me. Her long dark hair was pulled to the side of her head in a low ponytail, and she was wearing a pair of snug jeans and a baggy sweatshirt. It was the first time I'd ever seen her body so well covered.

"Well, come on in for crying out loud. How long you gonna stand here and study this door? He ain't in here, so you can't will him to walk out of it."

Beau wasn't here, either, but maybe she knew where he was. I hurried after her as she spun around and headed back inside.

The bar was different at three o'clock in the afternoon. The curtains were pulled open, letting sunlight inside, and the windows were open too, allowing a fresh, cool breeze to waft through the place, almost taking away the stench of stale beer and cigarettes . . . almost.

"He left yesterday. Ain't been home, neither. You messed

those two boys up good, girl." Honey shook her head as she wiped glasses off and hung them back up above the bar.

"I know. I need to fix it."

She shook her head and let out a hard laugh. "I reckon that would be nice, but the damage is done. Those boys about beat the shit outta each other in here yesterday. You've made them both crazy. Never thought I'd see a girl come between them two, but then I never figured you'd ever look Beau's way either. Once you started showing him some interest, I knew this was all going to Hell in a handbasket real quick. You've always been my boy's weakness."

I sank down onto a stool across the bar from her. My stomach churned with guilt. What had I done to Beau? How could I say I love him and hurt him so badly? Love wasn't selfish.

"I'm an awful person. I'd take it all away if I could. I can't believe I've done this to him."

Honey paused and raised an artfully sculpted brow. "Him who?"

"Beau," I replied, frowning.

A sad smile touched her lips and she shook her head. "Well, I guess he ain't as stupid as I thought he was. I figured the boy'd thrown everything away for some little gal looking to have a good time. I didn't think you'd actually care about him, too."

I wanted to get mad, but how could I? I'd done nothing to prove I cared anything about him. If you loved someone, you didn't screw up their life. You made it better. All I'd done for Beau was cause him to lose the one person he loved most in the world.

"Do you know where he is? I just want to talk to him. I need to fix this."

Honey sighed and slid a glass onto the rack above her head before meeting my gaze.

"No, Ashton, I don't. He left here after beating his cousin's face in. He was hurt and angry. I figure he needs some time, and then he'll come out of hiding. For right now you just worry about fixing your problems with Sawyer."

I shook my head. "There is no fixing my problems with Sawyer. He hates me. All I can hope is one day he understands, but I don't have time to deal with him."

Honey leaned both her elbows on the bar and studied me for a moment.

"You mean to tell me you ain't getting back with Sawyer at all? You ain't even worried about losing that fine future he planned on giving you?"

There was never a future with Sawyer. I'd known that all along.

"I love Sawyer, but I'm not in love with him. I never intended on forever with Sawyer. I just need to see Beau. The only dealing I want to have with Sawyer is getting him to forgive Beau."

Honey nodded and reached out to pat my arm.

"I think I might could like you, gal. Go figure. Me liking the preacher's daughter. Crazier shit has happened."

A smile tugged at my lips for the first time all day. She reminded me of Beau just then with her amused expression and the same hazel eyes.

"I need to talk to him. Please, as soon as you see him, tell him to call me."

Honey nodded and went back to wiping the glasses. I stood up and started for the door. The letter I'd written him during literature, apologizing and begging him to please talk to me, was in my pocket. The plan had been to slip it in his locker, but he'd never shown up at school. I pulled it out and turned and walked back to Honey.

"Could you give this to him when you see him?" I asked, sliding the folded paper across the bar toward her. She reached out and picked it up, meeting my eyes.

"Sure, darlin'. I'll make sure he gets it."

Both of my parents' cars were in the driveway when I finally pulled in well after five o'clock. It was time to face the music. No one met me at the door, which was a good thing. I stepped inside and was leveled by my father's penetrating stare. He was sitting in the recliner with the Bible open in his lap as he peered at me over his reading glasses. He was angry, hurt, and disappointed. I could see it all in his eyes. I dropped my purse on the coffee table and sank down onto the couch to face him.

"Glad you could finally make it home. Your brief text

message telling me you were fine and staying the night at Leann's wasn't exactly comforting. Your mother has gone to bed with a headache from the worry."

"I'm sorry, Dad," I replied. I truly was sorry I'd upset them. Even if I'd do it again in a heartbeat.

"Sorry, huh? Well, you don't appear sorry. I will say I'm glad you got to school on time and even made it to Grana's grave. Don't look surprised. I visit it daily, and I noticed the fresh rose on her headstone. Only you would bring her a single rose from her own rose garden. No one else would think of it. You're a good girl, Ashton. You always have been, but this summer something has gotten into you, and we need to straighten it out."

He'd blame it all on Beau if he knew. He wanted it to be someone else's fault. The fact that his daughter was one big fake didn't even register with him.

"Beau Vincent's missing too. Everyone thought you two'd run off together. But then you texted that you were at Leann's and her dorm counselor verified the information when I called and checked. So you weren't with Beau, but it is awfully suspicious that he is missing too and Sawyer has a black eye. What happened at church, Ashton?"

He was asking, but he didn't really want to know the truth. No father wanted to hear this kind of truth. I shook my head. "I got into an argument with Sawyer, and we broke up. I ran off to see Leann and get away. That's all I know." I was getting so good at lying. Not something to be proud of. Dad nodded and he closed the Bible in his lap.

"Good. I'd hate to hear you were messed up with the likes of Beau. Breaking up with Sawyer is probably a good thing. You two were too serious, and you have college coming next year. You need to be free of a boy so you can focus on your future."

He stood up and placed his Bible on the coffee table. His green eyes met mine, and he pointed to the book he'd just laid down. "Bad company corrupts good character. If you read your Bible more often, you'd know this."

I watched him turn and head for my parents' bedroom. I really wished he had hadn't made me hate to read the Bible. Having it shoved down my throat all my life had made me bitter toward reading it. I believed it, but my dad had used it to his benefit too many times and ignored the parts in there that would point out his wrongs. Like judging Beau without even knowing him. That was in the Bible too.

Chapter 22

BEAU

Beau,

I'm so sorry. For not calling you. For running off. For Sawyer. I've ruined everything for you. I was so selfish. I can't tell you how sorry I am. Just please forgive me. I can handle anything else if I can know you forgive me. Maybe what we did was wrong. Maybe we should have handled it another way, but I can't make myself regret any moment I spent with you. You gave me memories I'll always cherish. I won't make this hard on you. I'll let you go your own way. Just let me know you don't hate me.

I love you,

Ashton

I ran my thumb over the words "I love you" as I stared at Ashton's letter. She loves me. Ashton Gray loves me. I'd left her thinking this was her fault. The panic in her wording was clear. She thought I could hate her? Did she not listen to anything I said? Had my actions not told her enough? I'd sacrificed everything for her. How could she think I hated her? It wasn't even possible. The permanent ache where my mother had ripped my heart from my chest and basically thrown it at me eased some as I reread the words "I love you."

Right now I needed her arms around me so I could cry. Cry for the man who'd been the only dad I'd ever known and lost at such a young age. Cry for the brother who I'd never realized I had yet loved him anyway. Cry for the only girl I'd ever loved, the only person other than Sawyer I'd ever have died for, and the impossible situation we were in. I loved her so much. I'd chosen her over Sawyer, and I'd do it again. But things had changed now. Sawyer was facing the same pain I was. Maybe more so because it was his father, or our father, who'd cheated on his wife, ignored me my entire life, and lied to him. A tear rolled off my chin, and I quickly moved the letter away so my tears didn't smudge the words on the page. I needed to know someone cared. Someone loved me. Folding the note so I could see the words "I love you" and her name, I pressed it against my heart and lay back against a bale of hay. Tonight I wouldn't get much sleep, but I'd have Ash's words to keep me warm.

* * *

ASHTON

High school had always been easy for me. Having Sawyer as a boyfriend had protected me from harassment. As I stood in front of my locker and took in the word "slut"—painted in red nail polish across the pale blue paint that had gone unmarred the past three years—I had a moment of realization. I truly had no idea what high school really felt like. Maybe I was a slut. I wasn't a virgin anymore, and I wasn't married. Did that make me a slut? No one knew about me and Beau, so the fact I was being labeled a slut only meant they were hinting at it.

I sighed and quickly did my combination and opened my locker. I was instantly glad I didn't have ventilation holes in my locker. There is no telling what they would have tried to stick inside. I could hear whispers behind me as I pulled out my books for first period. No one spoke to me or stood up for me. Not that I expected them to. This was day three of "Shun Ashton." I couldn't really blame it on Sawyer because he wasn't participating. He wasn't standing up for me either, but he wasn't joining in on the fun. Everyone loved him and wanted to defend him. If ridiculing me made them feel as if they were accomplishing this, I could handle it. They were only words.

As if I'd spoken out loud, I was shoved into my locker from behind. The corner of the locker slammed into the side of my head, causing me to go a little fuzzy from the impact. I gripped the side of the door, praying I wouldn't pass out. Laughter of the female variety ensued behind me, and I closed my eyes until the pain subsided.

"Oh, for crying out loud. Are you just going to stand there and take this?" I slowly turned my head to see Kayla looking at me with an exasperated expression. She grabbed my arm to steady me.

"I get that you think you deserve this or whatever, but there comes a point when enough is enough. You need to stop them, or they'll continue to run over you. Get some teeth, girl." She took the books from my arms and closed my locker.

"Come on, I'm taking you to the nurse because you got a dazed and confused look in your eyes. Once she says it's okay, you can go to class."

I was dazed and confused. Why was Kayla helping me? She was head cheerleader. I'd have thought she'd be the ringleader in the anti-Ashton posse.

"You really should have thought about this before you decided to cheat on the town prince. Someone like Sawyer has too many loyal subjects. You've pissed them all off. They hated you because you had him for so long, and now they hate you because you hurt him. They feel vindicated in their brutality toward you. So either you get yourself a bodyguard or you get tough. This isn't going to go away overnight. This could last all freakin' year."

Kayla led me down the hall toward the nurse's office.

"I know. I figured I'd just let them get their anger out and maybe it would blow over sooner," I explained.

Kayla snorted. "Not gonna happen. Either Sawyer stops them or you do. Where's Beau? If he'd get his tail back here, he could stop all this."

I wanted Beau. I missed him. I reached down and touched my pocket to make sure the new note I'd written him last night was still there. I'd decided to take it to Honey this afternoon, just in case she was able to get notes to him. I wanted to make sure he knew how I felt. I didn't want him to be alone.

"Did you really do it? I mean cheat on Sawyer with Beau? I find it hard to believe Beau would do something like that to Sawyer. But Sawyer isn't talking, and Beau is MIA."

I wasn't going to lie anymore. Sawyer knew the truth. I didn't have his feelings to spare. Lying would be denying Beau. I couldn't deny him.

"Yes, I did."

Kayla paused, and I thought she was going to throw my books down or some other dramatic reaction, but she let out a low whistle instead.

"You admit it. Wow."

I shrugged. "Everyone knows. I broke it off with Sawyer. No reason to lie."

Kayla raised her eyebrows. "I can think of one reason to lie. The bunch of crazies who think they need to defend Sawyer by making you their punching bag."

"Maybe, but I'm not going to lie about Beau and me. He doesn't deserve that. I have nothing to be ashamed of except ruining their relationship."

Kayla opened the door to the nurse's office. "You really are unique. No wonder you got the Vincent boys fighting over you."

Other than an ugly welt on the side of my head, there was no damage, but I was beginning to wish I'd at least needed stitches so I'd had an excuse to leave school. By lunchtime I'd had my books knocked out of my hands so many times I'd lost count. Kayla had stopped once to help me pick them up, saying again how I needed a bodyguard. The janitor had cleaned my locker and the entire student body had been threatened with school suspension if caught defacing school property. So they had resorted to putting sticky notes with cruel comments on my locker instead. I stopped reading them once I realized they were just another form of punishment.

Sawyer had watched quietly as people had knocked my books to the floor all day. When our eyes met after I had cleaned off my locker from the latest onslaught of messages and he did nothing but walk away, I decided I might hate him a little. He wasn't the perfect guy I'd thought he was. Maybe I'd put him on a pedestal too. The Sawyer I'd known wouldn't have stood by while someone was bullied like this. My eyes had been opened to another side of him, one that was real but one I didn't like very much.

I was looking forward to getting a tray and heading outside to eat alone and enjoy some peace and quiet. Walking up to the lunch line, I ignored everyone around me. It had become my mantra to not make eye contact, but that seemed to make them all act worse. So instead I practiced tunnel vision, which was why I probably didn't see the Coke before it was poured over my head. I squealed as ice ran down my face and Coke burned my eyes. It trickled down my shirt and plastered my hair to my head. The lunchroom erupted in laughter. Nicole stood in front of me with her empty glass and a smirk on her face.

"Oops," she said loud enough for her audience to hear before spinning around on her heels and strutting toward her adoring crowd.

I stood there debating how to handle this. Kayla said I needed to get tough, but the fight was gone out of me. I just wanted Beau to come home. I reached up and wiped away the Coke in my eyes and smoothed my saturated hair out of my face. Then, without giving anyone the satisfaction of any reaction, I headed back to the double doors leading into the hallway. I could go home now. This was a good enough excuse.

The door opened before I could get to them and my eyes met Sawyer's. His blue eyes I'd once loved widened in shock as he took in my appearance. It wasn't his fault. Not really.

"Excuse me," I said as politely as I could, and stepped around him and headed down the hall toward the office. Even though I could feel his eyes on me, I didn't look back. Maybe this would be a final straw for him. Then again, maybe not.

Chapter 23

BEAU

Dear Beau,

I miss you. I miss your smile. I miss your laugh. I miss the way you look in a pair of jeans. I miss the wicked gleam in your eyes when you're up to no good. I miss you. Please come home. I think about you all day and night. It's really messing up my sleep, you know. I lay out on the roof last night and thought about all the nights we'd lain there and looked at those same stars. Back before life got all screwed up. Back before I chose the wrong Vincent boy.

Sawyer will forgive you. I think he's realizing what he and I had wasn't love. Not real love. He didn't know the real me, and I've found out I didn't know the real him. The things I loved about him aren't really holding up anymore. He isn't you. He never was. But then, there can only be one ridiculously sexy bad boy in town. I believe it's a quota thing. I'm teasing. You're not bad. You have so many good qualities. I admire you. I wish everyone saw the Beau I see. If they only knew how truly special you are . . . Please come home. I can't say it enough. I miss you.

I love you,

Ashton

She misses me. I want to go back and take her away. Snatch her up and run. Facing my uncle now, knowing he'd never once even tried to have any relationship with me, wasn't something I could do yet. I wanted Ash though. She could hide away with me. If I asked, I didn't doubt she would come. But I'd pulled her into an awful mess already. I couldn't hurt her anymore. She had the safety of her home; parents who loved her. She didn't need to lose them. They were important. They were a gift. Things I'd never had, and I'd be damned if I ruined them for her. Instead of turning on my phone and seeing the text messages she'd sent me, I tucked the letter against my heart and closed my eyes. For now this would have to be enough.

ASHTON

"Don't drop one. The damn things cost too much," Honey called from the kitchen.

I stood drying shot glasses and beer mugs before putting them away behind the bar. I'd started coming here after school every day to bring Beau a letter and see if Honey had heard anything from him. My frequent visits had started growing lengthy, so much so that Honey had started putting me to work. I had gladly accepted. This way I could talk about Beau to someone who would listen and not have to go home to my bedroom, alone.

"Tank takes five dollars outta my paycheck every time I break a glass. Knowing damn well and good those things didn't cost no five dollars apiece," she grumbled, walking back behind the bar from the kitchen, carrying another rack of cleaned mugs and glasses.

"I'm being careful," I assured her as I put the mug into the rack under the counter.

"Good. Now, tell me 'bout this locker business again," Honey said as she picked up a glass and started drying it along beside me.

"They're just putting sticky notes and ugly letters on my

locker, threatening me and stuff. It's silly. Other than the time I was shoved into the locker and hit in the head, I haven't suffered any injuries."

"And that sorry sonuvabitch ain't stopping them from treating you this way?"

I shrugged, thinking of Sawyer watching silently from a distance.

"He's just like his father. Don't know why that surprises me. Ain't gonna help none when Beau comes back. When my boy finds out Sawyer let this happen, he's gonna be spittin' mad. I was hoping them two'd mend fences once Beau shows back up."

"I don't intend to tell Beau about any of this. He won't know it happened, and once he's back, it'll have tapered off. That way he won't have a reason to be mad at Sawyer."

Honey snorted and slapped the bar in front of me with her towel.

"Girl, you grew up with Beau. You should know better than that. He ain't a dummy. Besides, someone'll tell him, and when they do, all Hell's gonna break loose."

I sighed and picked up the empty rack in front of me to take it back to the kitchen.

"I know he'll find out, but I want them to make amends. I won't ever forgive myself until they do."

Honey nodded. "Yes, well, my advice to you is stay away from the boys. I know you think you love my boy, but the Vincent boys are trouble. Both of 'em. They got issues you don't know about, and they need time. You'll just go messing up their heads. Besides, they run when things get tough. Beau's a prime example right now. Where's he at while you're being treated like a damn scarlet letter's tattooed on your forehead? And Sawyer ain't no better. He's letting a girl take the rap for all this and not saying a word. I love my boy, but he ain't the kind of guy you plan a future with. You need to move on, girl. Find someone whose last name ain't Vincent."

Since I was persona non grata these days, I decided it was in my best interest to bring a sack lunch and go hide in the library and eat. This way I was far enough away from Nicole and her soda to remain nice and dry. No one seemed to notice I was missing—either that or they didn't care.

With five minutes before the bell, I stuck my empty lunch bag into my backpack and headed toward my locker. The sticky notes hadn't tapered off any, which was surprising. I'd made it a point to avoid going to my locker except first thing in the morning and before going home. I just carried all my books around in my backpack. My body was aching from the weight, but I wasn't thrilled with the idea of turning my back on a busy hallway full of people who hated me. The bruising on my left shoulder from my book strap was nothing compared to being shoved into a locker face-first.

"The princess has fallen pretty low when she goes to hiding during lunch." Nicole's amused tone greeted me as I approached my locker. I slowly lifted my eyes to meet her glare. I wasn't sure why she detested me so thoroughly. Did she not think I had paid enough already for my sin against her? She stood directly between me and my locker. Stepping around her would be stupid. Instead I waited for her to say whatever it was she had come to say.

"How does it feel to be pond scum, hmm?"

I had to bite my tongue to keep from replying, "I wouldn't know; I'm not you." In a fight she would bash my face in. Besides, I didn't want to give her the satisfaction of seeing her words affect me.

"Don't ignore me," she said with a sneer, taking a step toward me. I stilled myself. The pure hatred flashing in her eyes was a warning to tread carefully.

"I just want to get to my locker, and then I'll go. I'm not trying to cause trouble."

Nicole cackled like some deranged witch. "You already caused trouble, bitch." She reached up and yanked on a strand of my hair, causing tears to sting my eyes from the sudden pain. "You think you're so pretty and perfect that you can just take whatever you want. Well, I got news for you, chick, you can't take what's mine."

Nicole closed the space between us and in one swift move, a shove to my chest, she sent me flying backward onto my butt. Great. I was going to get into a fight in the school hallway, and I hadn't even done anything. Just what I needed. My parents would be furious if I got suspended. Standing up seemed pointless. I kept my head down and waited for something else to happen. It didn't take long. My backpack was yanked off my shoulders, and books came pouring down onto my head. I cringed and let out a strangled cry as my head was battered by the heavy textbooks I'd been forced to carry around all day.

"That's enough. Move." Sawyer's voice silenced the laughter and chatter filling the hallway.

"Leave her alone, Nicole. Your beef is with Beau. Not Ashton. I don't want to see you touch her again. That goes for all of you. Back off. No one here knows what happened, and it's no one's business. Stop acting like a bunch of jerks and leave her alone."

Feet shuffled all around me and laughter had turned into hushed whispers as the crowd did exactly as Sawyer had ordered. The reigning prince had spoken. It'd taken him a week, but he'd finally ended this. His hand appeared in front of my face, and I stared at it a moment before ignoring it and standing up on my own. I didn't make eye contact with him, nor did I thank him. His interference was way past due, so my gratitude had expired. I began picking up my scattered books.

"Are you going to at least acknowledge me?" Sawyer asked as he picked up my backpack and opened it. I shrugged and barely glanced up at him before shoving my books into the bag he held open.

"You brought this on yourself, you know."

That was the last straw. I'd been a punching bag for five days too long. I snatched my backpack out of his hands and glared up into those blue eyes I'd once thought were so beautiful. Now they seemed pale and boring.

"No one deserves what I've been put through. I might have deserved your anger, but I didn't deserve the entire school's anger. I did nothing to them. So forgive me if I don't see how I brought a week's worth of relentless bullying on myself."

I spun around and started heading for the door. I was done for the day.

"Ashton, wait." Sawyer jogged behind me and reached for my arm. "Please, wait. Listen."

"What?" I snapped, not wanting my escape botched.

"I have something I need to say. Just listen, please."

I nodded but kept my gaze focused on the doors I so desperately wanted to flee out of.

"I've been wrong. Letting them do those things to you

all week and saying nothing was horrible. I'm sorry. I really am. In my defense, I'm hurting, Ash. I didn't just lose you; I lost my best friend, too. My cousin . . . my brother. Everything came tumbling down at once, and I couldn't deal. I told myself you deserved it, that you could fight your own battles. I guess I kept waiting to see the little fireball I remembered from when we were kids emerge. If I could see her, then I'd understand more why you turned to Beau. But you kept reacting the way my Ash would react. You never fought back or retaliated. You just took it. And God, that hurt so bad. They were hurting you. The girl I've loved all my life. I wanted to jump in and protect you, but the image of Beau touching your lips and you gazing at him like you wanted to eat him up flashed in my head and I became furious all over again." He let out a sigh, and his grip on my arm fell away. "I love you. I know the real you too. You think I don't, but how easily you forget that I was the one who bailed you out of trouble over and over again as kids. I didn't ask the perfect Ashton to be my girlfriend when I was fourteen years old. I asked the only Ash I'd ever known. You changed all on your own. I'm not going to lie. I was proud of the girl you had become. My world was complete. I had the perfect family, perfect girl, perfect future. I let myself forget the other girl you once were. Beau didn't forget her."

I swallowed against the lump in my throat. This was the

conversation we should have had as soon as Sawyer had come home this summer. Instead I'd run from the truth.

"I never wanted to hurt you," I replied as I stared down at my tennis shoes.

"But you did."

Chapter 24

ASHTON

One simple honest reply felt like someone had shoved a fist into my stomach.

"I know you hate me. I don't blame you. But Beau . . . Beau needs you. Please don't hate him, too."

I finally lifted my eyes to meet his gaze. A frown creased his forehead and he slowly shook his head. "I don't hate you, Ash. And I don't hate Beau. I wish he'd come back. When I left the bar Sunday, I didn't realize he'd make a run for it. I should have, but there was you, and I knew he wouldn't want to leave you."

"He loves you. He hurt you, and he can't face it."

A sad smile lifted the corners of his lips. "No, Ash. That isn't why he left." Sawyer glanced back at the now empty hallway. We were late for class, but I didn't care. I intended to go home, anyway.

"Come on. There's something I need to tell you," Sawyer said as he turned his attention back toward me.

I followed him outside to his truck. It was odd climbing up inside without him opening the door for me and lifting me up onto the seat. But somehow it felt right. This was how it should have been all along.

Sawyer pulled out of the parking lot and turned his truck south. Apparently, we were headed out of town for this talk.

"I went after Beau on Sunday. I knew I'd find him at the bar shooting pool. It's where he always goes to unwind. When I got there, we said a few things and threw a few punches." Sawyer glanced over at me and smirked. "I'd like to say Beau looked worse, but we both know I'd be lying. I might have the throwing arm when it comes to football, but he has me beat when it comes to throwing punches. Fact is he could have really put a hurting on me. He spent most of the time blocking my punches." Sawyer stopped and let out a frustrated sigh.

I hadn't seen them fight since we were ten and Sawyer accused Beau of being a troublemaker and dragging me down with him. Beau had gone to slinging punches that afternoon too. Sawyer had ended up with a loose tooth. Luckily, it was a baby tooth and needed coming out.

"My aunt Honey was there. It was just the three of us. She tried to break up the fight, but we weren't listening to her. Or, I should say, I wasn't listening to her. I wanted to see Beau's blood. You both had denied it, but I knew he'd kissed you. Heck, it's Beau. I knew y'all had probably done a lot more. I hated knowing I'd finally lost you to him. It was something that always scared me. Even when you two didn't speak much, he'd watch you, and when you thought no one was looking, you'd watch him. I'm not a complete idiot."

"I never thought you were, Sawyer. I lied about Beau, hoping to save your relationship with him. I fully intended to walk away from both of you."

Sawyer laughed, but the humor didn't reach his eyes. "You really think Beau was going to just let you go? Not in this lifetime."

"He loves you," I argued.

"I know. The thing is, he loves you more."

I started to shake my head.

"Ash, Beau wouldn't have betrayed me if he wasn't head over heels in love with you. No use in denying it."

"Okay," I agreed. Maybe he was right. I wanted him to be. "What did you bring me out here to tell me, Sawyer?"

Sawyer pulled over into a deserted parking lot and cut the engine. I waited patiently as he gathered his thoughts together. An empty plastic bag danced in the wind across the parking lot, and I watched it, thinking I knew exactly how it felt. It was on a path it couldn't control. So was I.

"Ash, Beau isn't my cousin. He's my . . . He's my brother."

I sat there as I let his words sink in. Did he mean in the metaphorical sense? I mean, I already knew he thought of Beau as his brother.

"I don't understand," I finally managed to reply.

"I'm still trying to understand it myself to be honest." Sawyer shifted in his seat and turned his body to face me. "When we were yelling at each other Sunday and saying things we really didn't mean, or at least that we would take back later, Honey informed us that my dad wasn't just my dad. But Beau's dad too."

"What?"

"Honey was my dad's high school flame. Then my dad went off to college and met my mom his first year in law school. She was the daughter of one of his professors. He fell in love with her and married her. Once he graduated and passed the bar, he moved back to Grove to open a practice. Honey was here still raising hell and breaking hearts, apparently. She and my uncle Mack use to hang out and stir up trouble together. So when she got pregnant with Beau and married Mack, everyone thought the baby was Mack's. My mom got pregnant with me the same year. She had no idea about Beau and still didn't until I confronted Dad right in front of her Sunday evening. Dad and Honey hooked up one night in a bar after he and mom had gotten in a fight over her spending too much money on furniture. They were drinking tequila shots, and Dad says all he remembers is waking up the next morning in Honey's bed. Six weeks later, she was knocking on his door claiming she was pregnant. He didn't believe her, and or at least he didn't believe it was his. So my uncle Mack married her. He believed her. Once Beau was born, Uncle Mack threatened Dad with revealing his night with Honey to my mom if he didn't agree to a paternity test. Dad took one. Beau was his. Uncle Mack said he'd raise him as his own. He was in love with my aunt Honey. Had been since high school. Then you know the story. He died. Honey was the lousiest mother on earth, and Beau was left to fend for himself."

I sat there staring out the window, unable to look at Sawyer. How could his father do something like this? He'd known how much Beau had suffered. I rested my forehead against the cool glass window and closed my eyes. Tears squeezed out and trickled down my cheeks. No wonder Beau left town. It was bad enough he felt unwanted by his mother. Now he had to deal with being unwanted by his father. Mack Vincent had only been his uncle. The only good memory Beau had of a stable life had been with Mack.

"Beau didn't abandon you, Ash. He just needs time to deal."

"Where is he?" I asked as a sob tore from my chest.

"I wish I knew."

Sawyer didn't say anymore. The truck cranked up, and we headed back to town in silence. I knew I should say something, but there were no words. Not for this.

Sawyer pulled up beside my Jetta, and I finally looked at him.

"I'm sorry. I know this has been hard for you, too. I understand now why you didn't say anything all week about what was happening to me. You have bigger issues to deal with than a little school harassment." I reached over and squeezed his hand. "Thank you, Sawyer, for telling me. For being a friend. For everything."

A smile tugged at the corners of his mouth. "There's no excuse for how I treated you this week, but thanks for trying to let me out of it."

"I understand now. That's enough."

He nodded, and I released his hand and jumped down out of his truck. This had been our closure, but the ache in my chest for the pain Beau was going through overrode the peace I knew was there somewhere. Sawyer was now officially behind me. He was my past. If only I could find my future.

Chapter 25

ASHTON

Honey's head snapped up the moment I stepped into the bar. I let the door close behind me while I studied the woman who had lied to her son his whole life about who he was. Over the past week I'd grown to like Honey. I didn't agree with her parenting skills, but I knew she loved Beau and that was enough. Now I wanted to see the remorse in her eyes, something to tell me she knew she'd done him wrong.

"Stop staring at me like I'm a damn science experiment. What's up your crawl today?" Honey asked as she stepped around the bar, holding my gaze. She was trying to decide what I knew. I could see her measuring me with her eyes.

"Why didn't you tell me the real reason Beau ran off? You let me believe it was me and Sawyer that sent him running."

She raised a thin, dark brow and sighed. "Guess Sawyer decided to share the good news with you."

"I don't consider the fact Beau has been lied to his entire life good news."

Honey pulled out a barstool and sat down, rolling her eyes at me as if I were being overdramatic. "What'd ya come here to do, Ashton? Scold me? Accuse me? Judge me? Go ahead. It ain't as if I'm not real used to that. But make sure you stop by your old boyfriend's house and give the same dressing down to Beau's daddy while you're at it. 'Cause, baby girl, it takes two to tango."

"I'm not here to judge you or any of those other things. I'm here because I'm worried about Beau. I wish you'd have told me. I would've gone looking for him."

"Wasn't my story to tell, now was it? Once I told them boys, it became their story. When they want someone to know, they'll make the decision to tell 'em. Not me. Besides, what's running off and looking for someone who don't want to be found gonna do, huh? Not a bit uh good."

I walked over and sat down on the empty stool beside her. Honey had known all along Beau wasn't hiding from his problems. He wasn't running away. He was coping with a life-changing bomb that had been dropped on him.

"Why'd you let me think he was running from me. From Sawyer?" I asked, watching her face for any sign of remorse.

"'Cause it was better that way. You ain't never gonna be

nothing but a wall standing between those boys, and right now they need each other. More than ever. I might not be an ideal parent, but I love my boy. I know he needs his brother. You're sweet and honest. I like you. I really do. You're nothing like I assumed. But you ain't good for them boys. They need you out of their lives so they can move on and find a way to deal with this."

She was right. I would always be the one thing standing between them ever mending their fences. I loved Beau. I loved him enough to let him go.

"You're right," I replied.

Honey reached over and patted my arm affectionately. "You're a good girl with a really big heart. Your mama raised you right. I'm thankful Beau has your love. It makes me feel good inside to know someone like you could love him. Thank you."

I stood up and wrapped my arms around Honey's shoulders. She stiffened then relaxed, and her arms slowly came around me. I wondered if anyone had ever hugged her. I squeezed her one good time before letting go.

"Thank you for putting up with me this week," I said with emotion clogging my throat. Her hazel eyes were misty as she gave me a sad smile.

"I enjoyed the company."

Before I became a blubbering mess, I gave her a small wave and turned to head toward the door.

"He's back in town. Just so you know. I gave him your letters."

I squeezed the brass knob and stared at the old wooden door. I had to let him go. Asking where he was and how long he'd been back would only hurt more. With every ounce of will-power in my body, I turned the knob and pushed the door open. It was time I went home.

The knock on my bedroom door was immediately followed by: "Ashton, sweetheart, are you in there?" I glanced at the clock on my nightstand. It was after eight o'clock. Dad was just getting home, which was unusual.

"Yes," I replied. He opened the door and stepped inside my room. The frown lines on his face looked as if he'd spent a stressful evening somewhere.

"You okay?" I asked, remembering the last time one of my parents had come to my room upset.

"Yes, I'm fine. I just want to talk to you about something," he replied, and took a seat in the purple chair facing my bed. This was apparently going to be a long conversation. He never sat down in my room.

"Okay," I prompted. His strange behavior was making me nervous.

"You and Sawyer broke up," he said it as a statement not a question. So I just nodded in confirmation.

"Have you spoken with him lately about anything?

Maybe something going on in his family?"

How did my dad know? Unless . . .

"Yes. Today as a matter of fact," I replied, waiting to see what his next question would be.

Dad cleared his throat and he leaned forward, resting his elbows on his knees. "What did he tell you?"

The frown lines and coming home late meant one thing. Dad had been counseling tonight.

"He told me something about Beau." I wasn't going to tell him Beau's secret if I was wrong and Dad hadn't just spent an hour with Sawyer and his parents.

"He told you who Beau's father is?"

I nodded slowly, unwilling to say more.

Dad let out a sigh and leaned back in the chair.

"Sawyer and his mother were in to see me this evening. They aren't dealing with this news well. But I'm worried about Beau. He's the one who I feel has been wronged the most. Do you know where he is?"

I shook my head.

"You'd tell me if you did? Because I really think he needs to talk to someone. Running off and hiding from this isn't healthy for him, Ashton."

"No, Daddy. Beau hasn't called me or come to see me since Sunday morning. But . . . he is back. Honey said he was back in town. He's seen her."

Dad nodded and rubbed his stubbly cheek, his eyes drawn into a frown. He wanted to help Beau. The idea of my dad helping Beau warmed me. I wanted to get up and throw my arms around him, but I stayed put. Beau wouldn't want his help. I wouldn't tell him that though.

"Is he mad at you?"

I shook my head but then stopped. I wasn't sure if he was or not. He hadn't sought me out. He hadn't called or texted. Maybe he was mad at me. Maybe he regretted everything.

"I want to apologize to you for the things I said about him after Grana's wake. I was wrong. I didn't know him. Sawyer has enlightened me quite a bit tonight. Beau had a difficult upbringing, but he has overcome so many things. I judged him unfairly. When he came to your Grana's wake and walked you up to the front it surprised me. It didn't fit the persona I'd labeled him with. A bad seed didn't do something so thoughtful for someone else. But it scared me. Beau was the son of a hell-raiser. I'd known Mack Vincent back in school, and he was nothing but trouble. I didn't want that for you. I was sure his father's blood had tainted him somehow. All this time he's had the blood of the town's most admired citizen running through his veins. Instead of taking care of what was his, he denied his own son. Mack loved that boy. I remember watching him with Beau and being amazed at the kindness he had with his son. The fact that Beau wasn't even his and he knew it only shows me once again how wrong I am. I was. The Bible tells us not to judge, yet I did anyway. I'm sorry for not trusting you. You saw the good in Beau that I refused to acknowledge."

This time I did stand up from my spot on the bed and walk over to my daddy. Without a word, I climbed up in his lap and laid my head on his shoulder the way I'd done as a little girl.

"It's okay, Daddy. I know you meant well. You were trying to protect me. But you're right. Beau is special. Somehow the neglect he has suffered hasn't taken away the spirit inside him. If you ever get to know him, you'll love him. He's hard not to love."

"Do you love him?"

"Yes, and because I love him, I'm letting him go. He can't be with me and salvage his relationship with Sawyer, too. I'll always be a reminder of his betrayal. I understand that."

Dad rubbed my arm and hugged me against his chest.

"I don't want to see you hurt, but you're right. I don't see another way. Those two boys have a lot of healing to do. They need each other."

"I know."

"But it still hurts," Dad replied.

"Yes, it still hurts."

Chapter 26

ASHTON

All night I'd slept with my cell phone clasped tightly in my hand. Just in case Beau texted or called. Yes, I was letting him go, but that didn't mean I wasn't worried about him. If I just could have known he was at home in his bed . . .

Today I walked through the hall without worrying if someone was going to shove me into a wall. The sneers had stopped. It was as if they all had something new to focus on. I wasn't the center of their attention anymore. Thank God. I turned to head toward my locker, and my feet slowed as my eyes landed on the achingly familiar body standing in front of it. My heart sped up as I took in the sight of him. I could now openly admire his butt in a pair of jeans. A smile touched my lips but quickly fell away once I realized what he was doing.

Beau was snatching off the notes still stuck to my locker from the day before. I'd grown weary of taking them off and with my confrontation with Sawyer yesterday, I'd forgotten all about them. Even though I couldn't see his face, I recognized the angry stance as he ripped up each note and threw it on the ground. Did he just growl? I took a slow, cautious step toward him. The tense set of his shoulders warned me not to make any sudden movements. He was furious and ready to pounce.

"Beau," I said his name gently before reaching out and touching his arm.

The last of the shredded sticky notes drifted to the floor from his hands. He didn't look at me. Instead he closed his eyes tightly. The tick in his jaw only made his sharp perfect features more intense.

"It's okay. The notes don't bother me," I assured him, wanting to say something, anything to ease his temper.

"He let them do this. I'm going to kill him." His words were so thickly laced with fury I started worrying for Sawyer's safety, again.

"No, he told them to stop," I explained, closing the space between us. Beau finally opened his eyes and turned his head. His hazel eyes, so full of emotion, studied my face.

"When? Because they sure as hell haven't stopped."

I slid my hand down his arm and laced my fingers through his.

"It doesn't bother me. Really. I don't care."

Beau snarled and slammed his fist against my locker door.

"I care. No one talks to you that way. No one, Ash." He turned and glowered at the packed hallway full of students. "No one!" he shouted. His hand pulled free from mine and the crowd parted as he stalked away. He was going to find Sawyer. I silently prayed he'd let him live.

Curious eyes watched Beau's retreating, then they shifted back to me. There would be no more letters on my locker. Beau was back, and I was positive he'd just terrified the entire student body.

The small pieces of paper at my feet were all that was left from my week as a social outcast. I bent down to pick up the pieces. Two scuffed boots stopped in front of me, and Toby bent down beside me.

"I'll help you. I don't think it was Beau's intention that you clean this up."

I smiled at him. He'd watched everything this week happen from the sidelines without saying a word. I knew he was only helping now because he was trying to find some redeeming grace in Beau's eyes.

"I don't want the janitor to have to clean it up. It isn't her fault."

"He's going to murder Sawyer if he finds out this was the least of what they've done to you this week."

I sighed, knowing he was right. If this made Beau angry,

then the nail-polish graffiti and the Coke incident was going to send him into a blind rage.

"I'm praying no one tells him."

Toby paused and studied me a moment. I could tell he was trying to decide if I really meant what I'd said.

"You don't want revenge?"

I shook my head and stood up, both of my hands full of paper.

"No, I don't want revenge. If this week was what it took to help Sawyer deal with everything, then it was worth it. Beau will never see it that way, of course."

"He'll end up blaming himself for leaving you here."

I dropped the paper into the trash can and dusted my hands off on my jeans before turning back around to face Toby.

"He had his reasons. Both Sawyer and I know that."

"So you and Sawyer made up?"

I let out a small laugh. Sawyer and I would never be completely healed. Too much bad water under the bridge.

"As made up as we will ever get."

Toby nodded as if he understood.

"And Beau?" he asked, looking unsure, as if he'd gotten too personal.

"Beau and I are friends." That was all he needed to know.

Toby nodded and slipped his backpack higher up on his shoulder.

"Sorry about this week. I should've said something. I kept waiting on Sawyer to step in."

"No worries. It's all over now."

"Beau's back," he agreed. Then, with one last apologetic smile, he turned and walked away.

I stood outside the cafeteria studying the double doors. Beau had appeared in literature class today, but he'd sat across the room from me and had not once glanced my way. I know because I watched him the entire hour and a half. Sawyer didn't show up to physics. There were no notes on my locker, and I'd gone all morning without a snide comment or someone sticking their foot out to trip me in the aisles in class. Only a few people actually spoke to me. It was as if they weren't sure how to treat me yet. Beau was ignoring me. It was impossible to miss. At some point everyone was going to relax and one brave soul was going to test the waters. I really didn't want it to happen during lunch. My lunch was packed and the library was upstairs, empty.

"You coming in?"

I turned to see Kayla standing beside me, her hand on the door. My heart rate picked up, and I decided no. I wasn't ready to face the crowd inside. I shook my head. "I don't think so."

"Why? No one is going to harm a hair on your head after Beau's performance this morning."

I wasn't ready to bank on that.

"What's wrong?" Beau's voice startled me, and I spun around to see him standing behind me with a territorial gleam in his eyes.

"N-nothing," I stuttered, and quickly stepped around him.

His hand reached out and grabbed my arm gently but firmly enough that I was forced to stop.

"Where are you going? The cafeteria is this way."

"The library. Ever since Nicole poured a Coke over her head during lunch she's been hiding out in the library to eat her food." The utter delight in Kayla's voice as she told on Nicole was obvious. I knew she wasn't telling Beau for my sake. She was telling him so he'd react. The fire that ignited in his eyes put a huge smile on Kayla's face before she twirled around and headed inside the cafeteria.

"You're not hiding in the damn library, Ash. If anyone even looks at you wrong, I'll fix them." Beau was staring down at me for the first time since this morning. I soaked up the little shred of attention. I was pathetic.

"Okay," I replied. Telling him no was impossible.

He reached around me and pushed the door open. "Let's go."

I walked in ahead of him and the entire room fell silent. This might possibly be worse than the laughing and snickers.

"Do you need anything from the line?" Beau asked, taking my elbow. I shook my head, scanning the crowd for any sign of Sawyer.

"Where's Sawyer?" I whispered when I didn't see him anywhere.

"At home. He has a concussion." I froze and stared up at him.

"What?" I asked horrified.

Beau's frown deepened. "He shouldn't have let them harass you. It was his mistake. He knows that . . . now."

"Beau," I said, jerking my elbow out of his grasp. This was why I couldn't have what I wanted. Because of me, Beau had given his cousin—no, his *brother*, a concussion. I couldn't let this keep happening. "Why would you do that? Is he okay?"

"He's fine. You can go check on him after school." He paused and clenched his jaw. "No, I take that back. You need to stay away from him. I'm not sure I can handle you worrying over him right now. I need time."

"Beau, I—"

"Go sit with Kayla. She's motioning you over. You're safe, Ash."

He turned and left me standing there watching him retreat to the far side of the cafeteria.

Chapter 27

ASHTON

I figured what Beau didn't know wouldn't hurt him. I'd sat in my room for hours, debating over going to check on Sawyer. Finally my conscience got the best of me, and I'd driven over here. Facing his mother wasn't high up on my list of things I wanted to do this year or possibly ever. I passed by his drive-way and turned down the dirt road leading down to the hole.

Once I got back there, I parked the car and sent Sawyer a text letting him know I'd come to check on him. If he wanted to see me, he would. While I waited, I figured I would go enjoy our favorite childhood spot one last time.

Climbing up a tree wasn't as easy as it used to be, but then our favorite limb wasn't as high as it used to be. It just took one small boost from the tree trunk to get myself securely on the limb I'd shared with the Vincent boys during our childhood.

"Impressive. You made it look easy." Sawyer's voice surprised me. I glanced over to see him leaning against a nearby tree. His dark curls danced in the breeze, reminding me of the times I use to watch with fascination as they did that exact same thing. I loved burying my fingers in his thick hair and wrapping his curls around my fingers. He really was beautiful.

"I was already here when you sent the text," he replied with an amused grin. My expression must have shown my confusion.

"Oh," I replied.

"To what do I owe this visit?" he asked, standing up and walking over to stand beside my legs. He barely had to look up to meet my gaze.

"I wanted to check on you. Beau said you had a concussion."

Sawyer chuckled and skipped a rock across the water he'd been holding in his hand. "He tell you how I got the concussion?"

"Yes," I answered him, feeling guilty.

"I deserved it. I was shitty to you all week."

Had Sawyer just cursed? "Um." I didn't know what to say. He was right; he had been, but he didn't deserve to be beat up by his brother over it.

"I shouldn't have let them do those things to you. Honestly, Beau beating the crap out of me was a relief. I'd been beating myself up. Having someone physically beat me was a nice release."

"What?" I asked.

Sawyer turned his blue eyes back up toward me.

"Ash, you were my girl for years. But before that, we were friends. The best of friends. I should have never let one snag in the road cause me to turn on you like I did. It was wrong. You took all the blame for something that wasn't entirely your fault. It was Beau's and it was mine."

"Yours? How?"

"I knew Beau loved you. I'd seen the way he looked at you. I also knew you loved him more than you loved me. You two had a secret bond I didn't get to be a part of. I was jealous. Beau was my cousin and you were the prettiest girl I'd ever seen. I wanted you for myself. So I asked you out, never once going to Beau first. Never once asking him how he felt about it. You accepted, and just like magic I broke up the bond you two shared. You guys never talked anymore. There were no more late-night roof talks and no more bailing y'all out of trouble. Beau was my cousin and you were my girlfriend. It was as if your friendship had never been. I was selfish and ignored the guilt until it went away. Only the times I saw him watching you with that pained, needy expression did the guilt stir in my gut. It was mixed with fear. Fear you'd see what I'd done and go to him. Fear I'd lose you."

I reached down and ran my hand over his hair. "I loved you, too. I wanted to be good enough for you. I wanted to be the good girl you deserved."

"Ash, you were perfect just the way you were. I was the one who let you change. I liked the change. It's one of the many reasons I feared I'd lose you. Deep down I knew one day that free spirit you'd quenched would fight to be released. It happened. And the fact it happened with Beau doesn't surprise me in the least."

"I'm sorry, Sawyer. I never meant to hurt you. I made a mess of things. You aren't going to have to watch Beau and me together. I'm stepping out of both of your lives. You can get back what was lost."

Sawyer reached up and grabbed my hand. "Don't do that, Ash. He needs you."

"No, it's what he wants too. Today he hardly acknowledged me. He only spoke to me when he was making a point to everyone else that I was to be left alone."

Sawyer let out a sad laugh. "He won't last long. He's never been able to ignore you. Not even when he knew I was watching him. Right now he's dealing with a lot. And he's dealing with it alone. Don't push him away."

I jumped down from the branch and hugged Sawyer. "Thank you. Your acceptance means the world to me. But right now he needs *you*. You're his brother. I'll just be a hindrance to you two dealing with everything."

Sawyer reached out and twirled a strand of my hair around his finger. "Even if I was wrong to take you without a thought to Beau's feelings, I can't make myself regret it. I've had three amazing years with you, Ash."

I didn't know what to say. I'd had good times too, but I did regret choosing the wrong Vincent boy. He gave me one last sad smile, then dropped my hair and walked away.

BEAU

Sawyer wasn't walking back to the four-wheeler he'd driven out there. He was headed straight for me. I should've known he'd felt me watching them. I didn't step out of the shadows. Instead I waited on him to join me in the darkness. Away from Ashton's view. My body was strung tight as a cord. When she'd hugged him, I wasn't sure I'd be able to keep from jerking him off her and hurling him into the damn lake if he so much as got close to her mouth.

"Did you see and hear enough?" Sawyer asked, coming up beside me to turn around and look back at Ashton. She was no longer watching Sawyer's retreat. She turned back to the water. The breeze played with her long blond hair, making my hands itch to go run my fingers through it.

"Yes," I replied, hating that he was as mesmerized by her as I was.

"She's all yours now, bro. We've found our closure."

I hadn't needed his blessing, but I knew Ashton had.

"From the moment I held her, she became mine. I'm sorry I

did this to you, but you never really loved the real Ashton. I do."

Sawyer nodded his head. "I know."

"I'll do whatever I have to in order to be worthy of her. She's everything I've ever wanted."

"Don't change for her. She made that mistake with me. She fell in love with you just the way you are. Just be you, Beau. Just be you."

She loved me. Hearing those words sent a shiver of pleasure over me. I'd finally won my girl.

"She had Mr. Perfect, and she wanted me instead. Doesn't make any sense," I said, grinning over at Sawyer.

He chuckled. "There's no accounting for taste." He elbowed me in the ribs. "Go get her, man. She's convinced she has to step out of our lives so we can fix our relationship. Her heart's breaking. I could see it in her eyes. She is ready to sacrifice her happiness in order to do what she thinks is best for you. Go put the girl out of her misery."

Step out of my life. Like Hell.

I slapped Sawyer on the back and headed out to set her straight. But first I was going to feast on those full lips of hers that were all puckered up in a frown.

ASHTON

Two arms wrapped around me. "God, you smell so damn good." Beau's voice was muffled in my neck. His warm breath sent chill bumps up my arms.

"Beau?" I croaked out.

"Mmhmm," he replied, kissing my neck and nibbling on my earlobe. I tilted my head to the side, giving him better access when I should have been trying to stop him. But with his warmth surrounding me and his hands moving up my sides, I decided I didn't care at the moment.

"What?" I managed to get out as his hands teased the lower portion of my bra strap. He was overwhelming me. I couldn't get my thoughts together.

"I love you, Ash," he whispered in my ear, and kissed a trail from my ear to my shoulder blade.

"Uh," I squeaked out. His thumbs brushed the underside of my breast and my knees started to buckle. It had been so long since he'd touched me.

"Easy, baby," he murmured, pulling me back against his chest as he leaned against the tree that held our special limb. His leg settled between my thighs and I trembled.

"I'm not letting you go. You're mine, Ash. I can't live without you." His voice was low and fierce as he held me tightly.

"But, Sawyer—"

"Sawyer is okay with this. I've spoken to him. He and I are working things out. But, Ash, I can't continue to want you from a distance. To love you and not have you. I'd end up in jail if anyone tried to touch you, and God forbid you tried to date someone."

I turned around in his arms and laid my hands against his hard chest. I loved his chest. Especially when it was bare.

"I only want you," I told him, staring up into his eyes. Those long black lashes shouldn't be so ridiculously sexy, but they were. Beau buried both his hands in my hair and sighed.

"Good, because I want you, too. Now. Forever. Just you."

The thought of forever with Beau sent tingles of joy through my body and shot straight into my heart. The dread and fear I'd felt when Sawyer had said he wanted to marry me one day had no place there. Because Beau was who I wanted. It had always been Beau.

Now that Beau and Ashton are hot and heavy,
here's a sneak peek at what's to come for Sawyer in:

the vincent brothers

LANA

Jewel flirted outrageously with the bartender. I knew her game and was willing to bet he did too. The brilliant scheme to flash cleavage and bat eyelashes while giggling wasn't the most original idea ever concocted. Why she couldn't just be happy with her soda while we waited for a table was beyond me. The ten-hour road trip I'd been on with her from Alpharetta, Georgia, to southern Alabama fulfilled my quota on quality time spent with my childhood friend and next-door neighbor. Jewel and I had grown up and become two completely different people, but that bond from our childhood had somehow kept us from drifting apart. Still, Jewel could only be endured in small doses.

"Come on, Lana, flash him a view of those fabulous boobs

you've finally decided to share with the world," Jewel whispered as her gaze stayed on the young guy fixing drinks for another customer. Shaking my head at her ridiculous request, I picked up my soda and took a sip. I was happy with my soda. If she wanted to make a fool out of herself in hopes of getting a mixed drink then fine, but I wasn't about to join in. The last thing I needed was to get caught with an alcoholic drink only thirty minutes away from my aunt and uncle's house. My uncle was a Baptist preacher and if he found out I'd been drinking alcohol, there was no way he'd let me stay with him and his family for the summer.

"You're such a party pooper, Lana," Jewel whined, and glared at my drink like it was offensive.

I didn't really care if she was upset at this point. I just wanted to get some dinner and then get to my aunt and uncle's. The sight of Jewel's taillights driving away was going to be a welcome event.

"I don't get you, Lana. You go and get all gorgeous and finally decide to flaunt what your momma—okay, maybe not your momma because God knows she ain't real attractive; how about flaunt what luck must have given you?—and for what? Nothing! That's what! You buy yourself a new, sexy, cute wardrobe and get a hairstyle to show off that head of hair of yours, but you *never* flirt. It's as if you did this for yourself and that's just dumb. Guys notice you now, Lana.

They turn their heads, but you just ignore them."

This was a familiar tirade of hers. It drove her nuts that I didn't throw myself at any boy who looked my way. I wasn't about to tell her the reason why. That kind of information would make Jewel dangerous. She'd find a way to ruin everything. She wouldn't mean to, of course, but she would. Her loud mouth always seemed to bring a world of trouble with it.

"I've told you that I'm just not interested in dating right now. We just graduated. I want a summer to prepare for college in the fall, enjoy being away from my insane mother, and just—relax."

Jewel sighed and bent her head down to nibble on her straw while her eyes zeroed in on the poor bartender who must have been about ready for us to be seated at a table.

"You can still come with me, you know. Skip this living-with-the-preacher stuff and come party all summer at the beach. Corey would love you to join us. Her stepfather's condo has three bedrooms and a killer view of the ocean."

A summer hanging out with a drunken Jewel and friends was not appealing at all. I had my plans, and so far everything I'd put into motion was running smoothly. But I couldn't help but be nervous about the next step. It was the most crucial.

Having my naturally red hair darkened to a deep copper and styled attractively instead of pulled back in a braid or ponytail had been step one. The darker red color had made my pale skin seem almost delicate. Then the cleaning out of my closet had been the next move. I'd bagged up every single piece of clothing I owned and dropped it off at the local Goodwill. My mother had been horrified, but after she'd seen the clothing style I intended to replace it with, she'd been very supportive. Unlike most mothers, my mother wanted to see me in shorts that showed off almost all my legs and tight tops that emphasized my c-cup boobs.

Jewel had wanted to teach me how to apply makeup, but I'd kindly refused and went to the Clinique counter at Macy's and had them teach me. Then I'd bought everything they'd used. Although I'd never been one for makeup, I had to agree that it did startling things to my eyes. I'd closed my bedroom door and stared at myself in fascination for hours after they'd put makeup on me.

Convincing my mother to let me stay the summer with my aunt and uncle had been a little more difficult. My cousin Ashton had helped tremendously with this part. She'd talked to her mother who in return talked to mine. Our mothers are sisters, and once my aunt convinced my mother that Ashton truly wanted me to come spend our last summer before college together, I'd been so excited I'd momentarily forgotten about the last step in the plan, the reason why I'd made myself moderately attractive and begged to come stay the summer with my cousin. The goal sounded so simple, but when I allowed myself to dwell on it then, it became so incredibly complicated. Getting a boy to fall head-over-heels in love with you wasn't easy—especially when he'd been in love with your cousin for as long as you could remember.

SAWYER

"You've got to curb the temper, man. If anyone could take on Beau, it would be you, but you'd still walk away beat-up," Ethan announced as I pulled out onto the country road from the dirt one that led back to the field party.

"It's been six months, bro. How long you gonna be pissed over this?" Jake asked from the backseat.

Why was this any of their business? Neither one of them knew what a committed relationship was like. They'd both been through so many girls during our four years of high school that I couldn't even name them all. Explaining to them that from the time I was twelve years old, I'd planned my life with Ashton at the center wasn't exactly easy. So instead I leaned forward and turned on the radio to drown out any more of their interrogations.

"You can turn on music all you want, but the fact is you got to let this go," Ethan said. "He's your cousin and your best friend. A chick can't come between that. Not for long." Ethan was watching me from the passenger seat. I knew he was waiting for a response from me, but I didn't give him one. His comment about Beau being my cousin was reminder enough that no one really knew me—except Beau and Ash. Beau wasn't my cousin; he was my brother. But once he found out the truth from his mother, he'd decided to keep that information locked away where it'd been his whole life. He didn't want to claim my dad as his own, and I couldn't really blame him. It wasn't like my dad had ever done anything to help Beau's home situation growing up. Beau held nothing but disdain for my father—*our* father. He chose to remember our father's brother as his dad. He'd been the only dad Beau had ever known. Even though he'd died when Beau was in first grade, he'd been a fond memory for Beau—unlike his real father.

"Hey! You passed Hank's," Ethan announced, pointing his finger toward the burger place where we normally went to eat.

"Not going to Hank's" was my only response. *They* were the ones who jumped in my truck. If they didn't like my need to get out of Grove, then they could walk back to town when we got to where I was headed.

"You leaving Grove?" Jake asked.

"Yep."

Ethan sighed and leaned back in his seat. "We may end up in Florida before he stops this damn truck."

"Florida? I'm starving, and a cheeseburger from Hank's would've fixed that," Jake grumbled.

Slowing down the truck, I pulled over and glanced back at Jake. "You're welcome to get out and walk back."

His eyes widened and he slowly shook his head. "No, man, that's okay. I'm good."

I pulled back onto the road and ignored the exchange between the guys. They both thought I was nursing a broken heart. Well, they were right.

No one said another word until I pulled the truck into the parking lot of Wings. I'd driven about twenty miles south to the next town big enough for decent restaurants.

"You should've told me you were headed to Wings. I'd have shut up." Jake made an excited whoop as he jerked open the back door of the truck and jumped out.

This was somewhere I'd never eaten with Ash. There weren't many places where I didn't have a memory of her, so my choices were limited. Tonight I needed to get my mind off her and focus on my future—or at least my summer.

"I'm gonna eat my weight in some wings," Ethan said in reply to Jake's excitement over my choice of restaurant. At least I'd made them happy. Not that it mattered.

Opening the door, I went inside and stopped at the hostess stand. A tall girl with long, blond hair pulled back in a ponytail smiled up at me with an appreciative gleam in her eye that I was used to. It had been habit for me to ignore that look in other girls' eyes for so long that I automatically brushed it off. Tonight I wasn't going to do that. It was time I started flirting back.

I flashed a grin that I knew was pretty damn impressive because it was the one Ashton always commented on. "Three please," I told her, and watched as her brown eyes got bigger and she blinked several times. She wasn't exceptionally pretty, but seeing her get all flustered was a nice balm to my ego.

"Oh . . . um . . . okay . . . y-yes . . . uh," she stammered, reaching for the menus and instead knocking them to the floor.

I bent down beside her to help pick them up.

"I'm sorry. I'm not normally so clumsy," she explained, two bright red splotches of color staining her cheeks.

"So it's just me then?" I teased.

A nervous giggle erupted from her, and I realized she'd never do. I didn't like giggles. Ash wasn't a giggler.

Handing her the menus, I stood back up and pointedly shifted my attention elsewhere. I didn't need to flirt with her anymore. She'd get the wrong idea.

"Okay, um, this way," I heard her say. Both Ethan and Jake quickly fell in behind her. I started to follow when my gaze stopped its uninterested appraisal of the bar to focus in on a female I would happily let giggle all she wanted.

Auburn hair hung down her back and curled on the ends.

Two very long, bare legs were crossed as she sat on the barstool and a silver, backless, high-heeled sandal dangled off the toe of a very dainty foot. I hadn't seen the face of this one yet but from the back, she was a head-turner. She had major potential.

"You coming or what?" Jake yelled, but I didn't turn my head to see how far they'd gone or where they were being seated. Instead I stood, frozen, watching her. Jake's loud voice caught her attention, and she turned in her seat and glanced over her shoulder toward him. Her creamy, smooth complexion was dotted with freckles. Normally, I wasn't a fan of a lot of freckles, but the bedroom look to her green eyes and the full, almost unreal-looking lips made it all work. She started to turn back around after seeing what the yelling had been about when she stopped and her eyes locked with mine.

Surprise, pleasure, and anxiety all flittered across her face as she studied me. I was fascinated. The bartender came up behind her and said something. She glanced back at him.

"Sawyer, man, come on," Ethan called out this time. Tearing my gaze from the redhead, I made my way to the table where the hostess was standing with our menus.

"Sawyer, wait." A familiar voice stopped me in my tracks. Disbelief settled over me as I turned back around to see the pretty redhead making her way toward me. As I made my way up her body, appreciating the view, I noticed a short, denim skirt that stopped several inches above her knees. The white top she was wearing tied at her waist in some sort of loose knot and small glimpses of a flat, smooth stomach peeked out as she moved. Finally I managed to get my focus off the impressive cleavage the shirt displayed in order to see her face. A small smile tugged on those ridiculously plump lips and recognition dawned on me.

No fucking way.

"Lana?" The incredulity in my voice was unmistakable. The last person I'd expected to see was Ashton's cousin. The fact she was the girl I'd been checking out was even more shocking.

"Sawyer," she replied, a full grin on her face.

"What're you doing here?" I asked, thinking more along the lines of *What the hell happened to you?* She looked nothing like the girl I'd seen about seven or so months ago. That girl had been sweet, prim, and proper. This one in front of me was a walking sexual fantasy.

"Eating," she quipped, and I realized I was smiling. A real smile, not a forced one, for the first time in months.

"Well, yeah, I kind of gathered that. I meant, what are you doing here, in southern Alabama?" She pressed her lips together and then her tongue peeked out and nervously licked them. *Hmmm . . . I wouldn't mind tasting those lips either.*

"I'm staying with Ashton this summer. My friend is

headed to the beach, so she's dropping me off at Ash's after we eat."

Ash. Damn. Did she have to bring up Ashton? My good mood evaporated, and once again I was forcing a smile. She glanced over my shoulder at my friends' table and frowned.

"You guys are already seated at a table?" She shot her frustrated gaze over toward the hostess stand. "Figures," she muttered. I followed her gaze and saw the blond hostess watching us with an irritated frown on her face.

"What's wrong?" I asked, turning my attention back to Lana.

She sighed and looked back at me. "We've been waiting on a table for at least fifteen minutes."

Ah. The waitress had given us their table. I could fix this problem.

"Go get your friend, and y'all come sit with us."

Lana flashed a bright smile. "Okay, thanks. I'll be right back."

I watched as she spun around and walked back to the bar. Her backside was impossible not to watch as her hips swayed gently from side to side. *Damn.* Lana looked good.

ABBI GLINES is the author of *The Vincent Boys* and *The Vincent Brothers* in addition to several other YA novels. A devoted book lover, Abbi lives with her family in Alabama. She maintains a Twitter addiction at @abbiglines and can also be found at AbbiGlines.com.